ANIMALS IN SUITS

Timur Raad

Copyright © 2019 by Timur Raad
All rights reserved.

ISBN: 978-1-7329-6160-9 (eBook)
ISBN: 978-1-7329-6161-6 (Paperback)

I thank God (S.W.T)

ٱلْحَمْدُ لله

I thank my Mother
I dedicate this book to my mom, Afaf, who is the greatest
individual I will ever know.
"Your Heaven lies under the feet of your mother."
The Prophet Muhammad (ﷺ) [Ahmad, Nasai]

And I wish the best for all people, creatures, and things
"None of you truly believes until he wishes for his brother what
he wishes for himself."
The Prophet Muhammad (ﷺ) [Bukhari and Muslim]

CONTENTS

Introduction

The alarm clock blared, "BEEP, BEEP, BEEP," with the green time displaying 5:30 AM across the ceiling panel. Jake swung his paw into the control pad and rolled back into bed, recognizing innately that the week had dragged through the day of recovery, and that another day of drudgery was surely upon him. Biological and organic evolution had generated transformation, extinction, and four billion years of all sorts of "intuition" of appendages, into pre-set habits. In the time before evolution of current technology, an alarm might not have been so manufactured, and the noise of a more dangerous predator screeching or natural disaster rattling might have generated the same response to that ancient "BEEP, BEEP, BEEP." Regardless, the danger of tardiness brought on the threat of scolding, and, if repeated, a worse outcome—relegation to the Chamber of Values where one was met with "therapy and rehabilitation." That opinion would be delivered by the overseer, the Box-On-Top in the octopus-like organizational chart of command, and supported by the Bureau of Humane Restraint (formerly Humane Retribution), but everyone called it HR. Whatever the result, a meeting with HR or the Box-On-Top (used to be known as B.O.S.S., and you don't want to know what that stood for) always seemed to have the same effect of being swallowed by some ancient beast, even on a false alarm.

Jake laid flat in bed for a few minutes shifting over to the right, then hanging over to the edge of the bed, staring across the room. Moving around the room was akin to being in perpetual close-quarters combat. The clutter in a small space made traversing to the kitchen, bathroom, or doorway a dance. One step around the path of untouched manuals, piled clothes, awkwardly crunched desk, cabinet, and multiple light globes in lieu of central lighting took its toll. The room ultimately doubled as the living room, guest room, kitchen, substitute exercise center, and whatever else it could entertain.

Now it was 5:35 AM; who else would be awake? What was the routine for the day? Eventually, the half-day would be over. The seven-day, 52-week, 365-day cycle of productivity persisted. The impending workday always arrived without fail. Jake knew no other life; he was bred for this one. Ironically, he spent half his free time thinking about work. There had been stories passed by elders to their progeny in communities where animals reveled in cities, villages, and farms. They were more mobile, more organic, and more aware, but as time went on, those memories faded. And what did those old timers know, anyway? Rumor and reality were inconsequential, and as many of the stories passed between people were lost, so did their authenticity, and the lore of the elders was forgotten. They were stored by the remaining seniors a few centuries past, but the periods of Incorporation and Vision destroyed what they could and relegated to confidential vaults the remaining relics and memories.

Growing up, Jake was one of the last broods born of natural birth. Born in facility c829.314.431 in the 51°31'00.1"N Latitude and 9°55'00.1"E Longitude region, he'd passed every health, speed, strength, trainability, and loyalty test. His productivity potential was high, and his health chip was light green across the board. Occasional irritation related to any pressures near the top of the paw was a reminder of the devices embedded there. The device had multiple functions entertained, monitored, and maximized one's health for the ability to work.

There were some rare offspring still produced outside of a facility. They were culled if tracked by the Bureau of HR and were reminders of a more chaotic time and what it represented—folklore and myth, "families" (just imagine that, people who like you just because. How silly!), estate ownership and things like "avocado toast" (what genius invented avocado toast?). The Incorporation and Vision era took that ever shining, ever blinding light and desire, and effectively refocused creation to its true purpose—to serve, work, and then work some more.

Jake was one of many worker drones, created solely for the purpose not of doing good or being loved, but to make more money. Profit was God, and every creature on earth its servant with a few HR representatives/Emissaries/Prophets/Visionaries and a Box-On-Top sprinkled somewhere in between. Jake glanced in the mirror before he left, slowly rubbed his eyes, and carefully ignored the urgent desire to scratch underneath his left leg (an instinctual holdover habit from before his training in the facilities).

Chapter 1:
Day 1

Ah, the week of productivity, back already. Always back. Always Monday again. Monday was the new Friday. Friday the new Monday. Did it matter? The day of recovery, whose purpose was to rejuvenate the mind and body of the organic being passed quickly as always, its benefits evaporating into the air. Jake got up and dragged himself over to the bathroom, slowly passed through doors, and stood in front of the sink. He waved his paw under the sensors, set it under the outpouring water, padded it across his face, and then waved it under the sensor again to shut off the water. Jake waltzed over to the closet and squeezed his shoulders into another ill-fitting work shirt, covered it with a jacket, and tried not to get fur all over his clothes.

"Badge...badge, where was the badge?" he panicked. "Uniform incomplete without the badge." He started pacing around as if that would make the badge magically appear. No badge meant no jump access, no work, and no purpose. GROWLLLLLLLL! He slumped down on the ground for a moment and was now eye level with the badge—it must have fallen out somehow! He exited his studio running on all fours, (the most convenient and rapid way, although he would get slightly sweaty) and slid the badge into the hyper tube entry. He waved his badge and shot over to the office.

Although Jake didn't ever want to go to work, it was the only constant in his life. One's devotion to work, if lacking in spirit, is never lacking in attendance. One had to go. Wants were only for various biological necessities—sustenance, food, and sex. Spiritual needs were much more muted. Desire was suppressed. The only drive that mattered now was the drive to be productive, not to produce, but rather to persist through work. Was work a marathon or a race? Or was it a crawl? Who knew? Maybe both. He had to fulfill his role in the corporate pyramid. As to the void that existed, that was what work was for. Corporations could have thousands upon thousands of laborers, but only handfuls of true owners…errr…"leaders." That's what they liked to be called. Owners implied some serfdom and ambivalence, an involuntary selection of position (which it was). Ultimately, that language of serfdom was abolished as the leaders found that terminology insulting.

One internalized the feedback loop where you would punish yourself (aha, take that corporation!) before the corporation could punish you. Quite ingenious. Every so often, the capable would make it to the top, but that was more coincidence and exception than the norm. The skill in ruling, conquering, or being elected to leadership was a combination of being lucky, having the right birth (born into the right tube with the right genetic heritage), and most commonly, cronyism. Those in leadership were selected through cronyism and favoritism rather than fate, merit, or any semblance of leadership capability (aside from 'skills' like being able to mete out punishment without any compunction, setting up meetings, and delegating work). Add a dash of ego and a sprinkle of some boot licking (now of course, no one in leadership would ever wear boots; this was just a figure of speech, as simple, plain boots were a ghastly sign of menial labor or military uniformity. A leader's footwear tended toward the outlandish—the rarer the material that covered

13

the feet of the leaders, the more powerful the leader. Diamond-studded moccasins, moccasin-studded diamonds or argyle toe-fitted shoes, the more fantastic the material the higher the status of the leader). Take Rachel, one of the managers. Her peacocking performance and plumes would magically appear only when the executives were around, her shoes monstrous in their adornment and bursting with feathers from other creatures. Otherwise, one would have imagined her an overly smelly fowl. Flashing her plumes and crooning were reserved only for the executives. The iridescent coloration, the eye-spotted tail came out only for a big shot—and all we peons saw was the stinky eye glare.

Speaking of the devil, what worse luck than the transportation tube spitting you out next to Rachel at the start of the day. Eye contact was made, too late! Rachel slowly bobbed back and forth towards him with one eye swiveling around inspecting the rank and file around her. Rachel rang out, "Goodddd morning Jake…Good morning!!!" Jake paused. "Yes, morning." Rachel quickly detected a bit of reluctance in that declaration, so she pressed on. "Yes, morning. Now how was that day of rest?" Ah, she made that horrible, and awful invocation, 'How was your weekend? (or well day of rest now, that the weekend was reduced from two days to one).' This was one of the innumerable, disinterested, and generic questions that one would get assaulted with upon entering work. Jake responded, "Ah, you know, a bit of errands." Rachel paused in her barrage of silly questions. "Errands" usually stopped them, or at least inspired disinterest. It was such a boring answer. What could they ask after? "Which pair of underwear did you wash? How was taking out the trash?" Jake had to leave to reach his desk. He started walking backwards while talking slowly, letting the volume die down. He waited until he hit a corner, and then he dashed down the hallway. He marched to his desk and sank down into his seat, letting gravity do all of the work. He breathed a sigh of relief, having escaped Rachel's scrutiny.

Jake hadn't been seated for more than a minute when an alert popped up on his arm pad, 'Late to meeting...' and while he was reaching paw to device, before he had a chance to dismiss it another, alert pinged him, 'Jake, get going...YOU ARE LATE. Have a nice day'—where was the employees cease and desist right? Even the device seemed to be snippy...and really it was Rachel's fault, forcing conversation. He walked over to the elevation tubes and entered, waved his badge over, and was sent to floor 295. The floor itself wasn't exceptionally memorable—cheap paints seemed to be the only things to hold the walls together and a generic bland wallpaper covered its' corners. Desks were strewn about, or zigzagged across, the hallways and stale carpet odors remained despite the newly installed cheap laminate. Here and there, crisp lights and occasional modern art prints supported the paint in holding the wall up. Of course building interiors could come in many varieties—Jake had occupied many places of employment and those many places of employment most certainly occupied Jake. Even when he left work, thoughts of deadlines, experiences of grievances and the stench of the day lingered. After he closed his eyes in his unit, he could sometimes still see the painting mounted in the hallway emblazoned upon his inner eye. At least the stench of the day could be rubbed out with a cleansing bath, although overcooked foods in the kitchen tended to cling more than the generic cleaners he used to sanitize his space.

In Jake's vast experience of bland corporate work spaces, building designs often had two consistent laws. The first was that that the time elevation tubes took to depart and arrive was always the same—which was forever. The second being, whoever you were trying to avoid somehow would appear waiting on the other side of those elevator doors. But how else could you get someone to the middle of the building? He'd move down the aisles in a familiar fashion, and land at his desk. He put his paw forward into the scanner and activated his program.

Science was still searching for a complete elixir for biological frailties, such as nutritional needs and removal of waste as well as a solution for emotions, their distractions, and any other physical or psychological barriers that interrupted productivity. The irony was the latter could be fixed without technology; just give the employee a better, freer life. Not everything in life was a problem or a challenge that needed to be solved. The corporation wasn't one to be stopped by the logical nor the rational and would create problems on its own. With enough packaging, separating, marketing, or re-aggregating, the consumer would be confused into submission and consumption, not understanding what or why they were consuming. The lines of supply and demand were controlled; there was too much food, too little medicine, and never enough shiny things. The response was always to make more or less of everything. Supply and demand sat on one side opposite of species psychology, and somewhere in between or outside of logic and rationale for what should be made, and that's when the problem generation machine would take place. The solution factories would then go to work making more products and services to solve these problems. Loops within loops would be created from consumption.

Some corporations were so powerful that they had militaries. Some had islands, and most had coffee machines. The corporations said that in mythology, co-ops lead to corporations because you'd cooperate for the betterment of everyone. It sounded like a re-write. There was no time for introspection, and even if there were, what would one reflect on? With what energy and what reference point (i.e. was one's existence relative to all species, to a small cohort across time, or to oneself and the dreams of oneself)? The artificial career ladder, the worksheets, code, and product...was there silent time or a time to pause long enough to step away and think about purpose, life, and the non-monotony of existence (the inverse of work)? Metacognition, or thinking about thinking, was one of the only escapes and reminders that introspection might actually exist. Artificial intelligence couldn't do that, nor could a zombie or robot. *"I do exist,"* thought Jake. *"I could do that. I can think about thinking!"* It also felt like the only personal layer not penetrated by the corporation.

Well, at least you still were a number. Imagine what it was before. Jake was employee 4,030 of 41,457 employees at BLC Corp., which was one of a thousand subsidiaries of a bigger subsidiary that was one part of several monopolies. There were limits for oxygen, nitrogen, and nutrition for all organic creatures and the environment, but there was no natural or real limit to the growth of productivity or profit. In history, you were told the stories of the founders—an apple was picked, packaged, and sold, and trees were planted endlessly. Then different apple products were made, such as frozen and sliced apples. Then there were pictures of apples, models of apples, and apple paintings. Eventually, artificial apples were produced and campaigns were launched to argue for their replacement of organic apples. At some point, one couldn't tell the difference between the artificial and the real, and what was organic was long lost, and the only thing that seemed to continue was the apple brand, it charged ahead for apple suits, computers, and so on.

Laws were a necessity. We were told we were the inheritors of the corporation's legacies, its laws, and its vision for the world, which was how that apple was picked, packaged, and consumed. The quasi-governments disappeared. The quasi-corporate governments moved in. The corporations took over. When corporations' revenues equaled that of an entire government, that might have been an early sign of the transformative change in the way of life. We were taught in history books about the age of countries, which gave way to the age of companies. At one point, ten companies were equivalent to 180 countries. Eventually, countries would cease to exist in their more official form, although some shadow governments remained in place. Twenty-five companies now had total revenue of $924,294,194,514. We could keep going, but it was a lot of units, and more than any country in history could have imagined! Oh, to even get a little bit of that unit action. The ratio of things was monstrous in size and audacity—14 billion creatures on the planet and 25 companies.

Fourteen billion on the planet and 5,014 owners with 49,422 trillion products created, as well as 14,192 trillion services rendered, 4,020 billion refunds, expired warranties, and so on. Good thing we had accountants and analytics departments to keep track of this stuff. The only thing left to count was employee bathroom breaks and a counter in the snack room. Countless lives gone, moments gone, epochs passed, and the interesting thing was how, despite retirements, the number of employees increased ever so slightly. History never remembers the individual employee. There was the employee of the month and the year, but they all faded to obscurity, recorded in some lost record book in the Inconsequential Hall of Employees. Jake wandered through the security gates, which were loosely and ceremonially guarded. He threw up his paw to brush against the scanner while holding his badge to activate the tube to floor 942. The tube spat him out to the floor. The office was always well lit and split into a maze of chitter chatter and break rooms with the occasional constructive corner. The beginning of the day involved various meetings, coffee ingestion, and snack consumption while hunched over operating stations. Jake walked through the parroting of, "How was the weekend?" the howling of, "You have a minute?" and the screeches of, "The pain, the horror…the fax machine is down!" He finally arrived at Desk 346, which was wedged between 347 and 345 ½ (there was a bit of space between the two). At least no Box-On-Top yet.

Chapter 2:
The Box-On-Top and the Boxes Lying/Laying/Lounging Around

On the organizational chart digitized in every system and tagged with every employee's ID, everyone was just a box. This chart encapsulated the hierarchy of the whole company. You ever stack a bunch of things, just grab something, and pile it up on top of something else? What if those things that ended up on top landed there out of pure luck, due to the elements, the thinness of their exteriors, or because some were different colors or dimensions, some had more content than others, and some less? Although it seemed random, the position of boxes had less to do with science than it did with relationships and enforcement. The content of the boxes was all the same, and their input and outputs were very much the same. The only different thing was the placement, which was itself often random. The outputs were commands, orders, and punishments, punctuated with occasional rewards. The inputs were driven by updates, which consisted of groveling, fear-pandering, and occasional treats. The only thing that distinguished the boxes was position, and the moment you removed everything from under them, things fell apart. More specifically, the position of leadership, of being the Box-On-Top, came with the title and belief that distinguished the Box-On-Top from the employee; that belief that you were superior or placed on this earth to delegate and denigrate. The Box-On-Top was merely a box on top of other boxes, no lesser and no greater than any other.

While there were many boxes on top of boxes, at the very top ruled the Biggest Box-On-Top (formerly known as 'The CEO', "He Who Drags the Golden Parachute", El Jefe Grande). Below the Biggest Box-On-Top were Junior Boxes-On-Top, Middle Boxes-On-Top, and the lowly employee was, appropriately, at the lowest rung on the ladder. A Box-On-Top would make clear the separation that existed between them and the employee (fear of punishment and shame were their main tools for motivation). Management's relationships with each other were taped together by status and titles. More importantly, what brought management together was the ability to feel no guilt, no shame, and no remorse in delegating all manner of work to the employee. The employee was stripped of their natural dignity, and subsequently clothed in corporate attire. The cruelest aspect of this was that the Boxes-On-Top knew their role was not necessarily to manage the employee inasmuch as it was to exhaust them. The order of things was that the managers would delegate work all the while extending, stretching, exhausting, breaking, pestering, harassing, and otherwise using the employee. This was what counted as management—the slow depletion of the soul. There were synonyms for Box-On-Top, such as Director, Managing Director, Senior Manager, Manager, and Vice President. These were the terms they saw fit. Some employees preferred to use terms like slave-master, fool, and dictator. These more appropriately described the relationship between manager and employee than the innocuous titles of Manager, Director, and Managing Director, which revealed nothing of the substance of the role. The role itself entailed constant surveillance, assessment, and deployment of different control devices.

One of these Boxes in particular, a veteran of many years and a VP, would casually stroll in with all sorts of pads, pods, tablets, and other devices. As he walked, the devices' lights were green, their notifications going off—*beep, ping, blink, tank, took, tak*—all while the Box swung his head wildly. He would *clip clop* clumsily around. People learned to be wary of his long neck. He was also infamous for his inability to stay still, always craning his neck awkwardly to look at everything, and snapping it back and forth as if a demolition ball was attached at its end. He was both awkward and authoritative, ungainly and dictatorial. His great height, long legs, and long snout gave him a goofy aspect, but despite his foolish visage, he was in charge.

To be in charge and to lead were wholly different concepts. Leading in the abstract was like anything else in the abstract. It worked; everyone was equal, resources were plentiful, and all enjoyed a world of complete agreement. In practice, things broke down and broke down fast. Those who followed the leader, also known as servants, employees, serfs, or whatever you wanted to call them, were motivated by fear of consequence and, on rare occasion, by hope of variety or reward. The Box-On-Top would wander, gallop, meander, then *clop* clumsily around the aisles muttering about tasks. Jake and his colleagues would feign interest, making haste—this was protocol. Smile. Look happy. Be thankful. Smile. Look happyyyy. Be thankfulll. Stay busy. These mantras were repeated so often in so many different ways that they became embedded in the minds of all low tiers. Incidentally, the Box-On-Top at Jake's company had a name: Cluster. To some employees, such as Jake, he wasn't Cluster, but Cluster with a four-letter expletive for all the chaos he wrought on others. To some employees, he was their savior and leader. A slight few employees were indifferent. Cluster had polish and shine. He was a proud beneficiary and dispenser of nepotism, but the skill in which he most excelled was mismanagement.

He was famous for his meaningless queries. Cluster hummed and snorted. One of his devices wasn't working. The devices were ornamental at best and distractions at worst; collections of tablets with applications running, monitoring software, tabulation engines, spreadsheets, presentations, and other digital liabilities. He paused for a minute. One of the employees, Patacakes, an unremarkable fellow, asked him, "You okay?" Cluster ignored him. He grabbed the device, and in a constipated shoveling towards the sky, shook it. His eyes twitched. Two minutes passed. It felt like Cluster had lost a loved one. His eyes squirmed, and he stared at the device until it finally started humming. Green! On! Cluster exhaled and looked calm again. He folded his long limbs and lowered his long neck into his lap to examine his manager's toolkit.

All managers had a calendar, a task list, and the authority vested by the Box-On-Top-Of-Them (basically, their boss). Not much else was needed. To be a Box-On-Top, some training could help. There were trainings on every topic that might pertain to the social and emotional life of work. For instance: how to deal with the unruly employee, how to make the employee produce, how to measure the employee's productivity, satisfaction, and risk points. There was also the micro-managing style, macro-managing style, and the hybrid approach—micro-manage the employee and then step back and tell them what the bigger picture was as well. Employees were trained with classical conditioning: ring the bell, let them salivate, punish them, and occasionally reward them. There were also general rules post meetings, and a follow up meeting, and follow ups to the follow ups, ad nauseam. Attendance at meetings was of paramount importance, as was monitoring. If you can't see them, they ain't working. There was a training program on the computer that trained new management and refreshed veteran management on Box-On-Top-Employee interactions. Cluster powered it up and brayed, "Computer begin training simulation!"

Employee #43: "Sir, I would like the day off."

Cluster: "Certainly not"

Employee #43: "Thank you, Sir."

Manager Simulation: Manager, 100 points, Employee, 0 points

Employee #13: "Sir, I heard we are possibly downsizing, is that true? I heard we might not get our holidays units."

Cluster: "From who? No—we are growing! And of course, some changes will be made…."

Employee #13: "Is it true that that the clients and customers want more?"

Cluster: "We need to step up our efforts, son"

Manager WARNING: Employee becoming disengaged

Cluster: "We value your input and feedback"

Employee #13: "Sir, we …"

Cluster: "Damn it—computer off"

Manager Simulation: Shutdown in progress

Program Terminated. Cluster had enough. Ungrateful employee. Time to get to the real thing. The warm up was enough. Dealing with real employees versus simulations was much more satisfying. Real employees squirmed more and showed pain more sincerely. Boxes-On-Top liked sincerity when it agreed with them.

Cluster approached Jake. "I would like an update, Jake." The game of tennis had begun, except Jake's paws were tied behind his back and his available responses were limited to dodging, navigating a quagmire of incorrect or dangerous answers, or guessing.

Jake: "Yeah, update. Update on the automation and efficiency project? Or forecasting revenues? Or finding ways to reduce cost, or…?" *Quick, Jake, think, just respond!* his internal monologue prompted him. "Yeah, on the automation and efficiency project," Cluster responded. Cluster started squinting. Silence. "And?" Cluster asked. Jake started becoming a bit irate. "Well, which project do you mean?" Cluster said, "We just need to make sure you're thinking about what we're thinking about." Silence ensued.

This wasn't Jake's first dog and pony show. It was more like his 15th. He had 12 bosses, 498 colleagues, and 25 different locations, but the one constant throughout was the eventual fading of the soul, the shortening of the temper, and the feeling of entrapment in something. Or maybe just plain ol' entrapment. The embedded paw chip didn't produce enough reverse cortisol. Jake banged the side of his arm pad and meditated on Cluter's use of the word "we." Who was "we?" Was it a word always used in communication to create the image of a conjoined, unanimous, democratic effort? Did the other management actually discuss this project or was this a power play by Cluster to further pressure Jake on the project? Regardless of the rationale behind the queries, there wasn't much room for choice, so Jake lobbed the ball over the net squarely at Cluster. "Yes, I will keep working on the project and responding to any other feedback." Jake's head performed a deferential nod of acknowledgment while his brain imagined him in a plane flying far away.

The posturing involved in communication between employees and managers required a large dose of acrobatic magic. Cluster had to repeatedly lean in with hands around the table. "So, we are on the same page?" he asked. *Why lean in?*

Jake thought. *Why not just try to strangle me directly?"* Jake careened backward. "Yeah." A fog of pain was coming over him. Life will not stop for you. Time will not stop for you. You have to step back and get your balance back. Get your focus back Jake, his brain asserted. Jake's pep talk didn't work. Cluster couldn't even let Jake's thoughts go unanswered. "Jake, one more thing," he whined. Jake responded, "Yes?" Cluster said, "Watch Joey." Jake was confused. "Joey? Watch?" He began to sift through his mental catalogue of Joeys. Did Cluster mean Joey with the white tail or Joey with the decorated fangs? Cluster said, "Joey from Desk 294. You can learn from him! Be more like Joey or at least Joey-ish." Joey from Desk 294 was the one with the white tusks, on a squat, sturdy body, covered in hair, boorish to some and oinking too often for others. Jake tried to hold back the feelings of indignation and anger running through him. He wanted to say something, but he had to survive. "Uhm, yes, Cluster."

To be compared to another creature was to have your uniqueness quashed, and furthermore, it was to place you in a position of constant comparison in which you always came out the lesser. Chocolate ice cream was better than vanilla and that was that. Forever more you knew you were vanilla: flavorless, colorless, at least to this individual. But flavor and taste varied by person, no? Cluster continued, "See how he smiles? How he does his work? He gives us his day of rest even. Ask yourself not what the corporation can do for me, but what can I do for the corporation. Got that Jake?" Jake reluctantly relented. Cluster sheathed his blades of punishment. This was just a warning. Any signs of self-defense or aggression on Jake's part would create issues for Jake far greater than the momentary loss of dignity. "Yes, I will try to be more like Joey." The sad truth was that *feelings* of losing control would soon be followed by *actual* loss of control. The rationalization never worked past the moment for

Jake. He did what he had to, but the weight on him was still there, oppressing him, diminishing him, negating his very self. Belief (forced or self-perpetuated) had this weird effect where it changed reality on occasion. If one repeated that belief, negative or positive, it could tear down or build up the individual. The compounding and drumming of words via imagery through the eyes, nose, and skull, until it housed itself in the coils and turns of the mind, actually distorted the mind. The repeated drumming and poisoning of the soul was quick, but curing such poisoning took a lifetime. "Be like Joey."

Images of Cluster appeared to Jake. And who was Cluster? Who was Joey? Cluster could have been worse. Jake had seen worse, but why is he not being treated better? Jake's pad started beeping, alerting him of the upcoming event. Looks like it was time for the dreaded quarterly HR meeting. Cluster waited outside the door a bit. Zach was shuffling towards him. Cluster closed the door, and it looked like he was pointing at Jake while he was out. Jake thought nervously, *And what? Is Zach now going to watch me? Like learn from me, be more like me?* He just laughed and kept walking. Next, they will have Joey there and Cluster asking him to watch me, but it'll be a different type of "watching."

Chapter 3:
"Do more with Less. Freedom Within Limits...Oh and Sacrifice"

Everyone shuffled, flocked, or swam in an orderly manner to the large auditorium. There were various rules referred to as Values and Principles; essentially, these were commandments to all employees. The rules were the rules. That is, until the rules were changed by a vote from the Chief Box-On-Top and the Council of Boxes. Meetings were held quarterly for employees to go over these rules, and they were given copies for their desks and homes. They were also given plenty of swag. Swag was the name for numerous company-labeled and approved trinkets distributed to employees to show appreciation. They were so cheaply made that they likely were retainers of negative value. And yet, they had an attractive characteristic; they were free. The crowds responded to the loudspeaker announcement: "Get ready for someeee gifts, goods, and swag!" Employees were given black bags and bins to put away and carry their swag.

The first bins of swag, containing shirts with "You are the best!" "BLC united" "BLC runs on love," pens (no one used pens), and key chains (no one used keys either) were ready. All manner of appendages were flying up to grab, gobble, and attach to the swag being shot off the stage into the crowd. Keepsakes were important and physical reminders of BLC. One associate screamed with happiness, "I am the best!" HR chimed in to another HR, not realizing they were near the loud speaker, "It's just a shirt." The crowd went silent. Another HR figure quickly grabbed the microphone and yelled out, "We love you! One BLC!!!" He scurried over to the event coordinators and urged them to move ahead of schedule, and then he started firing the second avalanche of swag at the audience. Trinkets were trickling in, coffee mugs were flying, employees were swerving, and umbrellas spearing through the crowd.

There was the incident a few years back when some poor intern was not only speared, but also had a mug crack their head in two. Abayomi, Lou, and Belinda were huddled together. Feathers were flying, their beaks pecking at whatever they could reach. They were part of the frenzied scramble to catch the swag. Their green necks and grey coats worked side by side. Some cruel fellow fowls would label them the common Dove, and although the label "common" was apropos, Abayomi, Lou, and Belinda were also uncommonly greedy. Abayomi flew into some event marketing flyers. Lou swung right for two mugs and yelled out "Got em!" Belinda was running around the floor scrounging for any and all pens that hadn't been crunched by the stampedes of adrenaline driven beasts.

The corporate announcer pulled up the presentation on the screen, grabbed the loudspeaker, let the euphoria die down and began, "Are we ready for the review?" The crowd cheered back, "We're ready!" Jake muttered something. They began reviewing the commandments:

1. No through Yes
    a. "You don't say no, you don't tell us what to do...."
2. Integrity through integration
    a. "Integrate first, then have integrity"
3. Respect through restraint
    a. "Never talk back, show respect"
4. Democracy through dictatorship
    a. "Democracy after allegiance to the dictator"

5. Equality through elitism
   a. "Only the elite can distinguish equality"

To ensure proper education, the commandments were played wherever a speaker existed, but only on occasion. They were also randomly displayed on posters, on the bottom of cups, and inside break rooms. The display was random enough to create anticipation, but not so random as to be forsaken, excused, or forgotten. The commandments were intended to save the employee from themselves, (or at least that's how the Bureau of HR explained it). Humane Retirement had two goals. Firstly, retiring ineffective employees, those who were estranged from the commandments or otherwise piqued and had no more use. Secondly, supporting the Box-On-Top. Now, ineffective didn't necessarily mean incompetent (although that happened occasionally). It meant estranged from the commandments (i.e. if you believe in saying "no', then you really aren't saying "yes,' are you? If you pushed back, etc).

Ranked in order of severity, at the highest level was breaking a commandment. For example, you could take someone and throw him or her over the side of the highest building or steal office supplies. One was worse than the other, but they were all equally better than breaking a commandment. There were rewards for ferreting out (no insult or harm to any ferrets committed) those whose constitutions were weak, those either explicitly or implicitly attempting to refute or challenge the commandments. HR kept naughty and nice lists, although the nice list was mostly for symmetry and was often empty.

Names started scrolling across projectors with room numbers. "Everyone, please start moving towards your groups and rooms. These sessions will be anonymous; a way to share candidly, and also a way to get to know your colleagues," HR announced. The HR representative turned the communication pad off, and one of the other representatives waived over a mix of individuals from the Legal and Compliance Department. "Hey listen. We are short-staffed today. You need to make sure this is all recorded and on the books." One of the individuals from legal looked perplexed and hesitant. "Uhm, wait, I thought we told them it will be anonymous." HR responded, "Listen, anonymous can mean many things." The individual from legal said, "Actually, no. It seems to be strictly defined." HR shot back, "Do your job. The employee wouldn't exist without the corporation, right? This is for the greater good. Let them emote. Protect the company. If there's a bit of protection left, throw it to an employee." HR then called to an individual from Compliance, "Hey you! Wait, I have a task for you." The low-level compliance analyst said, "Sure." HR said, "Watch legal."

Everyone had arrived at their requisite group sessions. *Group sessions, great,* Jake thought. Here he was stuck with Abayomi, Lou, and Belinda. This had to be a setup, to be stuck with a bunch of stool pigeons. Then Jake reconsidered. *Let me give them the benefit of the doubt.* "How are you, Abayomi, Lou, Belinda? Guess we are a group, eh?" Lou was the verbose one, "So I heard we are discussing values. Ok, my favorite value is mentorship." Abayomi echoed, "Yeah, values are a good one. Wait, or mentorship, good value." Jake rolled his eyes, "Belinda, want to add anything?" Belinda responded, "Wait, if we are doing addition, then who's doing subtraction?" *This is going to be a long session,* thought Jake to himself.

Everyone started walking out in different directions, and soon Jake felt someone following him. It was Zach, a cousin of sorts to Billy. He was related by subspecies, but his variety was from the highlands rather than the deep jungles. He had the same large build, same muscular frame, and most of his brethren and sisters ate roots and shoots. When no one was looking, though, Zach would chew on old boots (that was more a peculiarity than anything). He was not as kind as Billy. Quite the contrary: Zach was ruthless. The haggard Zach would wander around with an insane smile, pestering, spying on, and constantly peering at others' work and stations. Zach hopped around while chewing on some unknown crud that was orange-ish in color, matted, and smelled like rotten bark. No one dared ask what it was. Zach's advice to all employees, his trick, that is, was if you were asked if work was too much, you should respond, "Nothing I'm not used to," but it is amazing what you can get used to. Zach, of course, was likely fed this by management, and being an employee, it would make it appear to be collegial advice when it was really malicious in origin sprung from management. Ironically, Zach didn't believe it himself, but those made the best truths. He knew himself to be a liar, but was honest with himself about it. He'd take a bullet for management if they weren't already slowly draining him and drowning him in adages. Zach's other favorite line was, "Remember the old days," which he'd state when reminiscing. "The old days" might have been remembered more fondly by others, but the average employee would rather not remember them. The marginal cost for Zach's dignity was low, whereas for Billy, it was priceless. BLC Corp and others like it depended on the low cost of its many "Zachs" and careful avoidance of too many "Billys."

HR asked what the employees were doing, what their wants and needs were, and who should be on the list of therapy and rehabilitation. Here Jake made two mistakes. Mistake one was unintended proximity. Mistake two was engaging with an awkward and polite greeting. You had the feeling you couldn't win, neither being polite nor impolite made a difference in the whole, although the previous might grant the employee clemency. Regret crept in, and he thought, *When could I go back home?*

Building 41-604-13-4-13 was like any other complex, cramped and full of low-net worth employees, but sometimes the thought that anything short of prison was better than work would creep in to his mind. In prison, there was no fraudulence and hypocrisy. One was the criminal and the other the enforcer. No hidden formalities or appearances. Punishment was punishment, reward was the absence of punishment.

Zach had taken it upon himself to conduct an independent study of Jake. He had notes on various conversation times and dates of all sorts of individuals. Jake's name went on the list and kept moving up. There were rumors of Jake's discontent, and Zach knew this because he'd spread some of them. There was much for him to discover about Jake. What did he want and what did he need? Were his thoughts misaligned? Was he still in tune with the commandments?

Zach approached Jake and said, "How was your wee…?" Before he could finish, Jake interrupted him, "Wonderful. All rested, and happy to be back at the office." Zach started the onslaught, "Jake, do you have a minute?" Jake wanted to say, "no," but blurted out, "Ok" (Ok felt a little less soul-crushing and passive aggressive than a hard yes, but really, it should have been a no). Zach continued, "Jake, you need to appreciate where we are as an organic species." Jake said, "You spreading a rumor again?" Zach responded, "One rumor? There should be at least a few by now." Jake started scrunching his face, preparing for the unsanctioned and dubious interrogation. Zach continued, "We are taller, bigger, live longer, suffer almost no disease, and we don't have to go…" Jake was staring out the window. Zach said "Jake?" Jake looked over. "Yeah?" Zach angrily said, "Now where do we go from here? What is it that you don't appreciate about this setup?" Jake said, "I didn't say anything." Zach said, "Look Jake, I can see it in your face. I don't want to have to put you in a hole. You're at will. We all come here because we want to and *should* want to." Jake was thinking, *What puts Zach in a place to tell me what to do, how to think?* He acts as if he was a Box-On-Top, not that they matter either. What a bully. Jake wanted to snap, but fear and risk of retaliation held him back. Jake said, "Yes, makes sense. Listen I have to run to a meeting." He sped off using his animal strength and speed to escape, leaving Zach perplexed at his desk.

Chapter 4:
Some Work...

There was some work to be done. The great work generator would spit out assignments at random. The Box-On-Top would review and then allocate them based on loyalty, attire, competence, and other important factors. The competence factor had to be balanced. You wanted a moderately competent employee mixed with a wholly incompetent one. The result was not complete failure or success but instead an extension of the project and security of the system. The moderately competent employees would have to stretch themselves while the incompetent ones would just be themselves. Although you needed some projects to be successful, mediocrity was more often the norm. It wasn't without some fairness that every creature suffered from ineptitude: Boxes-On-Top, HR, employees, everyone. The distribution itself however seemed to reward ineptitude at higher levels more so than with employees. And the moment an employee was given even the slightest taste of power, or attention from management for a perceived opinion that mattered, that employee—ironically—instantly abandoned their history, their memory of pain and punishment, and eagerly embraced their enhanced position in the realms of management.

It took a lifetime to break an employee and an instant for them to forsake their previous position and sell-out. Not all, but most, Jake included, had to be careful about the trick of being included. Even if you were in front of the CEO, you were not included. Jake saw Mosef, who was quirky and, weaselly, but intelligent. Jake walked over to him and started talking to Mosef about his thoughts. "Mosef, what do you suppose...." Mosef cut him off. "Jake, do you ever stop babbling to yourself? They don't pay us for idleness." Jake responded, "Well, you haven't even let me begin talking. And if that's what pay is, I don't want to know what we'd get if we weren't paid." Mosef responded contritely, "We've heard it once, we've heard it a thousand times. What is the reason for this, or that? Just do your job, and it's not talking Jake. It's complaining. What rule is that? Don't forget rule #48: Do not make problems, solve problems." Mosef proceeded to throw out the multitudes of terms and phrases that normalize work—'chopping wood', 'staying proactive', 'be impactful', 'give it 110%' (I mean how was it even possible to go over 100%?).

For example, if you emptied a cup of water, was 10% more water going to magically appear? I guess maybe in the non-physical world, pain could be felt to 143%, or 2050%, but with work there was always the imperative to push harder beyond physical or natural limits. What was wrong with putting in 20%? If one even received units or payments, it was more like 1% of the work's' production value. The return on investment for the employee was 5% and 500% for the corporation. This didn't seem fair. What constituted enough? Enough to keep you busy, to subsist, and to maintain purpose.

Jake sarcastically interrupted Mosef at some point, "Be proactive, don't forget, its best to keep work on your mind at all times." Mosef didn't pick up on the sarcasm. "Yes, you got it, challenge yourself! Be a problem solver. Make impact. That's what HR calls it: impact, and as the grand Box-On-Top always said, leverage yourself, extend yourself!" he boomed. Jake had enough. He quickly turned and headed to his workstation.

He grabbed the earpiece set, put on the goggles, and started moving his gloves to weave and motion in the repairs. Mosef was his project partner on this. He was very tall, mostly volume and, little density, with tentacles and a jelly-filled belly. He had to operate within a water saline encasement (or else the his fellow employee would have to don a suit and enter a watery environment). Mosef worked more on the programming side whereas Jake was a fixer. He'd take hold of the robotic hands virtually and move them down the pipes to find where the problems were. Jake grabbed the screws, went into the guts of the device, and started moving around the screws. Mosef changed more lines of code.

The next generation of code writing robots was still being developed in the lab and not up and running, for now you still needed the Jakes, Mosefs and employees of the world. For now Jake had to create charts from the outputs because Mosef kept changing the code. They were both well onto achieving the ever moving KPI's (Key Performance Indicators) and project milestones. One of the project meetings was coming up. Mosef and Jake worked in tandem plugging in their receivers. The call started, it was the bringer of useless news. Eddwerdy said, "Soooo we have this timeline, that timeline...we have to meet this deadline for releasing the new code. Mosef, update?" Mosef, sick of updates, replied, "Yeah, uhm, code changed."

Eddwerdy was a scraggly piece of work. Neck stretched out, wings hitting his cubicle, and huge caruncle, snood, and wattle, "Look Mosef, we will need more specifics than that." Jake was preparing his next remark while this assault on Mosef's update was happening. Eddwerdy interrupted with a slew of charts and graphs, and graphs and charts. He screeched out, "We do a good job of this, and there's gonna be some units and fame coming your way." *Nothing like a false promise*, Jake thought. *Dangle the carrot and then beat with said carrot until they don't even want it. How many times has one delivered on their part as the employee only to be let down by the employer? Uhm, one, four, twenty...ok maybe one shouldn't count.*

Mosef snapped at him on the chat 'Pay attention!' sensing Jake's thoughts wandering. Jake snapped his attention back to the robotic hand. He was lucky Mosef was safe. One couldn't display such perceived disinterest without fear of being reported to a Box-On-Top or HR.

It was time for the next meeting. Communication pads lighting up, Mosef, Jake and oh God...Zach, Belinda, and Tse. He felt his blood pressure, heart rate, and breathing rate all rising. Mosef asked Jake on the chat, "You okay there?" Jake replied, "You could say that. Do we need this meeting?" Mosef responded, "Jake, the meeting is starting." Three beeps indicated each joiner on the compad conference.

Tse joined first, followed by the rest. Tse was the senior member of the conference by virtue of his status as a Box-On-Top. He began, "Ok, so everyone we are going to cover this demo of these new tools. They are going to be automating some artificial intelligence, data piping, reporting, machinery. Any questions?" It took about 15 minutes for Tse to finish the list. Zach asked, "AI? What do we need AI for?" Tse said, "Cheaper labor, more efficient processes, so the work will be done even more productively. We can now, as a species, focus on higher value stuff." Jake said, "uhm, like what?" Tse responded, "Well we'll have to invent what's next, but we have enough entertainment and consumption to keep our attention and take our time." Jake hesitated and then said, "Seems odd that we need to find something to keep the species busy." Tse sighed, "Greater profits Jake. Any more questions?" Belinda felt brave and threw a question out, "Artificial intelligence. Is that better than natural intelligence?" Tse ignored her question. Jake had to respond, "Do we have a choice as employees in the matter?" Tse and Zach, started laughing. Belinda imitated them. Tse said "In what? Besides, the decisions have already been made, and you are being informed of our path." He continued, "We're going to test out this artificial intelligence stream by having it monitor Jake and Mosef."

Jake interrupted, "Can we at least pretend to volunteer to have the machines learn our jobs?" Tse kept talking. Jake was angry. *How could they just treat us this way? I am sick of his domineering droning voice.* Jake repeated, "Tse, so no choice? When do we schedule with the robot?" Tse sensed the sarcasm, "Zach can help you acclimate." *How unfair to monitor Mosef and I, and task Zach with monitoring!* Zach seemed uncomfortable himself, "Tse, but I thought…" Tse cut him off, "Thought what? We can take this offline. There's plenty of promotable material here Zach." Tse said, "So Jake, do we have an understanding? You and Mosef make sure you turn on the AI programs when conducting work." He paused. "Listen, this will grow on you. It's a bubbly, straightforward process. Turn on the program and camera and do your work!" Jake said, "Camera! I have to attach a camera to myself?" Tse said, "No, not just you, Mosef as well will have to attach the camera, how else will we train the Robo…, err, AI." Jake didn't catch the last part or maybe Tse didn't finish it. Jake muttered to himself, "Maybe this Robot is more dangerous in my mind than in reality." He thought to himself, *what world is this that we are afraid to lose the jobs we hate?* What a cruel emotional swing from happiness into fear, fear into happiness. One day a machine could be doing this work; the question is should this work even be done?

There wasn't a shortage of types of jobs at the moment. Some folks started out at the bottom, and when you think about it, mostly stayed at the bottom. There were the loiterers, waiting to clamber up to higher levels. Their wait was in vain. There was the credit stealer, proactively sliding themselves in between someone and their work. There was the snacker/break room resident (a PhD in using break rooms). There was the stalker, bothering whoever they could. There was the organizer. The panderer. The overachiever, who was still incompetent. The true overachiever always exceeded everyone's expectations but their own. The talker, no question/comment/thought left not verbalized. The delegator (the worst). The micromanager (also the worst). The soon to be retired (to be pitied). The loud cruncher and public talon clipper (okay, the worst of the worst). There were more types, and ultimately, they all shared the commonality of the work and wasted meetings. Most could do presentations, spreadsheets, and complain. Could the Robots ever get to that level of sophistication, the AI, the automation? Probably not. To put together spreadsheets and presentations was a skill. Jake was finishing up one cell while fixing the wrong formula. Now to re-update the deck. Yeah, good luck having a computer do that. If it even wants to. If it gets a choice.

"Oh damn, I'm late," Jake thought. A one-on-one was coming up. He growled, then started running over.

Chapter 5:
The One-on-One

In another room in the office, some forgotten employee walked out. Ding, ding, ding! The wrestling match had begun. Lights were shining. Masks were on. Crowds...well, ok, no crowds. Cluster pushed through the door with bravado, his face frozen in his customary look of bewildered anger. To Cluster's surprise Jake was sitting there. Jake to his own surprise was there on time and beat Cluster to the room. Cluster was more of a Sumo Box-On-Top. He would just rush you—no finesse. Just drop weight, boulder roll, and swipe. Cluster began, "ahhhhem...ahemmmm." Pause. Jake thought, "*great, awkward silence.*" Cluster continued, "We also want to go through a quick surprise review Jake. How's that sound?" Jake said, "Uhm, great." Yes, who didn't like being reviewed? Who didn't like being treated like a punching bag? It was a range of subjective and objective questions. Interrogations? A surgical session to deconstruct the individual.

Cluster pre-ambled because he's a Box-On-Top; a manager had to pre-amble. "We are gathered here today, Jake, for your annual review. You know what time of year this is?" Jake responded, "It is..." he trailed off. Cluster cut him off, "Yes, we know what time of year it is, Jake. Don't get smart. Let's just start." He shoved the paper across:

Annual Review

Box-On-Top: Cluster

Employee: Jake Berlin

> Communication/Responsiveness = D-
> Work on: How many times do we have to talk to you Jake? We need positivity.
>
> *Quality/Timeliness* = F-
> Build out: The Apocalypse will arrive before you show up on time Jake (and that's IF the Apocalypse could make an appointment...).
> Jake—be early. Being on time, is just being on time, we want you pacing around, waiting for the meeting to start.
>
> Shirt Pressed = B+
> Keep up: Good job Jake, we love the shirt...
>
> Memorization of Company Values = D-
> Work on: Just sleep, eat, breathe, and poop company values. More "yes," less restraint. More bubbliness.
>
> *Knowing the Business* = C-
> Work on: We want you to know everything about BLC. You might not move up, or use anything directly—but we want you to have awareness. We need you to be able to mentor and coach the younger staff.
>
> Mentoring/Coaching = F+
> Work on: Refers back to "Knowing the business." Be careful when mentoring and coaching the younger staff.

Cluster continued, "Now, listen, let's get to the point: I've heard there's some disenchantment with the role. I've heard mutterings that Jake feels this, Jake feels that." Jake started opening his mouth while Cluster hammered on, "Work is a choice Jake. You're not forced to be here. It is a priority, and you MADE that choice. Jake, I care. The grass is greener on the other side, is it not? Listen, don't you want the five-year anniversary globe? You give us five more years, you get a globe!" he exclaimed. Jake wanted to say, "What the hell do I do with a globe?" but instead said, "Well, the thing is, who said that about me?" Cluster retorted, "That's confidential. It's a team, Jake—we behave like a team." Jake responded, "Well, if we are a team, how come I can't ask who accused me, and what kind of team is it if it's only a team of convenience and nepotistic and elitist hierarchy?" Jake couldn't stop himself, "And what the hell will I do with a globe?"

Cluster snorted, "What will you do with a globe? He asks me—what will you do with the globe? A gift of honor and service, Jake. You'll get to show the world your dutifulness and commitment. Are loyalty, commitment, and duty beyond your ego?" Jake was looking through the review, "Cluster doesn't this part on mentoring and coaching contradict itself?" Cluster calmed down and went with what was on his mind, "That's the review. Deliver, and we will reward you." *What the hell are deliverables, anyway?* Jake wondered. Things changed so quickly that the only constant was that term. Is there something that was actually physically delivered at some point? Disguising bureaucracy with busywork, busywork with non-work, non-work with labor, labor with the reward of a globe. It wasn't in Jake's power to decide what was necessary at work. Jake felt like time was the biggest loss in all this and that he was trapped in circles of thought that only led to dead-ends. Cluster stared at Jake and admonished him, "Jake? Are you daydreaming again?" He received no response. Jake was in a kind of hell, his mind wandering beyond this conversation.

Cluster yelled out, "Next."

Processing 1-1's by forming a line of employees was much easier than feigning any customized or special time. Everyone got a 1-1. Come and get it. Slippers was swimming towards Cluster, fins moving against the mechanical water driven pedals pressing against the ground. Cluster yelled, "Hurry it up!" Slippers started moving faster. Cluster chuckled, "Slip faster, Slippers. Get that?" Slippers blinked his eyes quickly. Cluster did his usual 180 personality flip and moved from chuckling to chomping his teeth in anger, "You spineless...slow...incompetent." Slippers waited. Cluster looked finished. Slippers went ahead and said, "Uhm, yeah, I am invertebrate." Cluster cut him off, "Yoouuu..." and slammed the door shut.

It was interesting to see how Cluster treated (or mistreated) different employees. Some employees, like Eddie and Kevin, made it by with vigorous bootlicking and shoe shining. Others, like Sardeep or Ari, made it by because they were non-threatening: weak and defanged/declawed or otherwise de-weaponized. As his friend Billy would say, "A strong enemy is better than a weak friend." It seemed preferable to just be a "strong person" than to have all the relativism implied in these empty platitudes. Billy explained it once in the following way, "A strong nemesis will force you to be stronger, a weak friend will allow you to regress further, unchallenged." Jake just never could appreciate this advice. It was like one of those meaningless corporate mantras: "Don't stress, just work harder." Sure, "don't stress...feel good, be the best you can be..." These mantras were obviously luxuries of the untested—"don't stress...feel good,"— they were laughable. Jake had a new aphorism, "Only dead fish will go with the flow." Slogans carried by Boxes-On-Top and occasionally repeated by bootlicking employees served the institution and the management, and they worked to sever the wits of the employee.

Cluster needed all these management tools of slogans, symbols, mantras, and empty language that he could find. This way, he could herd, mush, corral, and control the employee. As soon as any departure from established norms or trained behaviors was detected, Cluster immediately went about applying this arsenal in a methodical fashion, ultimately correcting the illicit and undesirable behavior of an employee. For management, the method varied but the secret sauce was pouring in fear, limiting reward, managing expectations and giving the mirage of purpose. Adopt this method, and you'll create a loyal employee. It was the loyalty of the fearful. The frustrating piece was a new employee would come about and they'd have to be retaught. It would have been easier to figure out a way to pass down the fear of management, but biology hadn't had enough time to adapt to that behavior. Biology had programmed fear of harmful natural occurrences. Fire—run from it. Cold—avoid it. To this list, we can add a new fear: Management—run *from and* avoid it.

As Jake was thinking of the most loyal employees and Boxes-On-Top, Formange came instantly to mind. Formange's thick shell glistened under the artificial lights, his long-shriveled neck and face emerging from its top. He had a huge body with small, stumpy legs supporting a hard underbelly. He was another Box-On-Top, and he and Cluster were friends of sorts. He sure did move slowly, and he had risen in the ranks slowly too. Employees used to joke that the tortoise beats the hare, and there sure were a lot of hares for Formange to compete with. He and Cluster were friends by virtue of status—the kinds of friends who were defined by the group that they were a part of. The lines of this friendship were blurred at times, altering because of competition over employees, but a manager was ultimately just a manager, and friendship served more than one purpose. Their friendship constituted an alliance, and they sometimes played the role of advisor, and on occasion, adversary, to keep one another sharp. Mostly, they shared a commitment to excess, and celebrated their ability to expense, punish, and manage things.

Formange was waiting for the room, and when Cluster came out, there was a smile and strong hoof-flipper bump between the two.

Formange exclaimed, "Cluster you old dog! How are you?" Cluster responded, laughing, "A dog! If you want to see a dog, you should see this one I'm working on. What a stubborn piece of…" Formange kept talking, "Hey, are you done with your one-on-one's? I need to break some staff." Cluster snickered, "You mean break *in* some staff or break bad habits?" Formange responded, "Oh, what did I say?" Cluster said, "Make sure you break in a few staff for me as well. Oh, some interesting information for you—the labs are still working on some tools to help us Boxes-On-Top, but jeez, if the staff would only cooperate more. One day, we'll have remote collars or tasers or something" (the audacity of where they believed their hierarchy was instilled!) "We'll have those ungrateful employees producing more and complaining less." Cluster and Formange started laughing. Cluster said, "Hey Formange, when do we get our promotion for all this work, eh?"

Despite the friendship between the two, there was still some competition between Formange and Cluster. Formange had been given indicators he might move out of the middle-manager Boxes-On-Topes to the top ranks. Formange just said, "Well, just wait and see Cluster." They were late. Meeting time—they both ran. Or rather, Cluster loped over and Formange crawled.

Chapter 6:
Break Time

Break time was a monitored activity meant for release and rotations of staff. The monitors were hidden within the walls and blended seamlessly into the room. This was for employees' safety, of course. The great trick in work was that you paid with your most valued asset—your time, always, your soul sometimes, and your health, often. At least you got free coffee, or a stocked kitchen, a new hat or a bag of chips, a bottle opener and if you did really well, sometimes units. These gifts were meant to offset the cost to your psyche. Units were nice; you could buy extra things with them from the company consignment stores: yellow umbrellas, green shoes, and avocado toast—how accommodating that you'd even get to buy things back from the companies you work for! So, you basically give them back the units that they gave you for things that you helped produce. Win-win for everyone. No one was ever sure where to pile up all their new yellow umbrellas that they got from work for free, but you never know when you'll need extras.

There was this story of the Great Don, who was really into work: he was a legend. He never left the office, never took breaks, and even gave up his Day of Rest just to come back to work. The Great Don was flightless, round, and slow, the last of the last of his species. He was big for an avian, with heavy plumage, but absolutely no ability to fly. All that was left of him was legend. One day, he was found buried in a landslide of all the yellow umbrellas he collected over the years. Rest in peace, Great Don.

Unlike the Great Don, Jake was not into work, or its complementary swag. Jake saw one of his friends, Billford Borneo, and walked over to him. Jake started talking about the new software installed and how miserably it worked. He told Billford how he might have to start training an AI, or a Robot or whatever they called it. He still hadn't gotten over his annual review. Jake tried to not fidget too much, to avoid the usual bouts of static shock he'd get (then again, having mounds of fur gave you static shock doing anything). Billford grunted his agreement. Billford Borneo had been part of the system for ages—Billford Borneo to everyone else, but Billy to Jake. His coat was gray, but his muscular frame still gave the appearance of youth. Intelligent. Capable. Hated banana jokes (ironic given the jungles his ancestors were from and all the simian jokes he had endured). He worked one division over from Jake's and maintained some small process that was part of a much smaller process.

Billy said, "You know Jake, I started using my time of recreation for a bit of exploring." Jake laughed, "Yeah 'exploring.' We all need to do that from time to time," and mockingly bounced around. Billy repeated with more emphasis, "Yeah, exploring, you heard right, so quit laughing." Jake was startled, "Why so gruff Billy? Your panel broken, and circuits gone bad?" Billy said, "Listen, there are ways to leave this place and see others." Jake looked around nervously, his imagination running, and responded, "What exploring, what's there left to explore?" Billy quickly responded, "You know, just going out." He paused for a moment, and then triggered by Jakes paranoia looked around and repeated in a low tone, "Going out, walking right out." Jake asked, "Walking out to where? There's nowhere outside of the complex and offices!"

Billy started to say, "There's a ..." when they heard something. In the background was the sound of someone clucking and shuffling towards the break room. The Box-On-Top, Tse from the nearby cubicle farm, apparently felt the need to surprise some unlucky individuals in the break room, and the poor individuals happened to be Jake and Billy. "Gooddd evening Billford Boreno. Jake, Jakey—how was the weekend?" *Here we go again*, Jake thought. "Wonderful Tse!" Jake gave Billy a quick glance suggesting it was time to end the break. Billy started walking backward. Jake walked over to grab coffee while talking to Tse to give Billy time. Tse started the prodding. "How are you liking work? Your team? Boss, any new updates?" Jake knew enough not to talk. "Coffee is great!" Tse looked annoyed. "But how's the team?" Jake had a moment of truth (well more like a moment of lies). "Uhm, yeah, great!" Any answer was the wrong answer to Tse, and more words compounded the problem. Once the tribe of managers and HR loyalists labeled you and pointed you out, you were quickly branded.

The response to this was to feign loyalty, reduce the appearance of intelligence, or act confused (although such a behavior would be discovered eventually). *One should almost never give the truth to the untruthful*, thought Jake. Tse pressed one last time, with some bait. "Ah it's hard work though sometimes, no? I feel like it's challenging work." Jake didn't fall for the bait, "No, seems like enough work. Speaking of which, I have to run," and Jake escaped. "Nice try, Tse" Jake snickered under his breath as he scampered away from the room.

Far from the break room, another employee was taking a break. Joey had been floating around in the back. He had a muscular neck, large but slow-moving legs, a hard shell, and a long snout. He was the type of committed employee that gave it his all, though his motivation wasn't pure. He was far from being robotic and believing in the Commandments blindly; rather, Joey was more a selfish survivalist with enough belief in the system to make it work for him. He knew if he worked with the system he could get to where he wanted to be. Maybe even be a Box-On-Top one day. It did happen. Rarely, but it did.

He was given one particular project by Cluster that he remembered clearly. In a one-on-one Cluster told him, "Joey, I need you to monitor, errr..mentor someone...on second thought, just monitor. I'll take care of the deconstruction, you just monitor." The slippage between mentoring and monitoring went unnoticed to Joey, although it hinted at the relationship between the two. He continued, "It is painful for me to point this out. But they are just not getting along with folks. Their work seems to be lacking. They give me a headache..." Joey interrupted for a second, "Who?" but Cluster trudged on, ignoring the question. "One more thing, you want to be promoted? You want to be recognized, right? Stick to what I tell you, Joey." Cluster enjoyed hearing his own voice, "So listen Joey, we can give you knowledge, rank, prestige, recognition, units. We can give you this, that, and that over there." Cluster pointed to the 'Employee of the Year' award, and cleared his throat. "But Joey, you watch, note, and be ready to identify the behavior that we see." Joey said "Who...? You mean note the behavior, right?" Cluster said, "The behavior WE see." Joey was a bit confused, "Wait, doesn't that mean you've already made up your mind?" Cluster said, exhausted, "Just do some sleuthing, and keep tabs."

Spotting Jake interrupted Joey's thoughts, so Joey walked up to him. "Jake, how are you?!" Jake said, "Better if I can run off Joey. Let's talk in the hallway." Joey stepped out with Jake, "So, yeah, save me from Tse. Can't even catch up with a friend without getting interrupted!" Joey responded, "Tell me about it. This place makes you wonder sometimes." Jake had to gripe, "Well, what choice do we have." Joey responded, "Not much. So who were you meeting with? How's Billy been?" Jake said, "He's good. You planning any vacation, Joey? I mean, not that we can actually take vacation, nor that there's anywhere to go, but it's fun to plan." Joey responded, "There's a few holo programs I'd love to try, but apparently, they still don't work completely. Hey, I gotta say Jake. I'm glad we're friends. Can't find a lot of trust worthy folks these days." Jake chuckled, "Tell me about it. I have to keep Zach off my back. I swear I think someone from Legal was even peering into a peer group session." Joey's face turned red and drool starting moving across his fangs. Jake said, "And you know what Joey? One more thing. If I hear one more time how lucky I am to be here, I'm going to barf." Joey teasingly said, "Woof?" Jake said "har, har," and responded, "I even had Zach trying to feed me some of this. 'We are lucky to be on the team. There's a long line that wants to be part of this group,' blah blah. Sure, I get it. Our ancestors had to survive war, famine, and disease. We just have to survive a 9-5, 6 days a week, but 9-5 might as well be a war wrapped by disease with a little side of famine. It's a slow demise, with no glory." Joey looked at his arm pad, it beeped a command—"I have to run," he said to Jake. "Late for a meeting." They both took off.

Chapter 7:
The Meeting

After break time and a slew of one-on-ones, the most important event of the day came: a meeting. There were meetings between employees, meetings between HR and employees, meetings between HR, and finally, and most important of all, was the meeting between the Box-On-Top and the employee. At least for Cluster, Tse and any other Box-On-Top these types of meetings induced the best feelings—they could just taste it, smell it, and feel it: the delicious anticipation. In preparing for these meetings, Cluster was known to have euphoric flagellations; these meetings were the orgies of the uninitiated, unwilling, and underwhelmed. The only guarantee was his coat was fluffed with excitement. For the employee, it was a fleeting, painful, anxiety-driven competition to the bottom, with chances to pander, grovel, and kiss up in all of its disgraceful flavors while simultaneously losing more of your soul in public.

Very rarely was a meeting to share useful information. That might happen more by accidental alignment of interest from attendees and intelligence from the presenter, with an actual convergence of articulation by all. There was as much chance of all those variables falling into place as all the planets aligning on a single connecting line followed by a massive solar eclipse; it was an extremely rare occurrence. Cluster was often a groveling shameless panderer that arguably embarrassed the establishment at times. However, the establishment was never one to correct mistakes, and any affairs not interfering in the grand scheme were accepted and ignored. The meeting was quickly approaching. Oh, the anticipation of the glorious time! It was the core reason for Cluster's existence. He'd had some one-on-one fun. Now it was time to have his fun with everyone as group.

Cluster entered room A-4-V2-16-11-IV, back erect, head hitting the entrance as would often happen when he clumsily waltzed into the room (that long neck was not helping matters). Everyone was seated and waiting. Cluster had a peculiar set of habits, not one but many, and his most dominant habit—over obsessive focus—was easily mistaken for a state of perpetual seizure. His long hind legs folded, and after much awkward flailing, he finally was seated. On rare occasion he spouted sounds that amounted to some type of articulation, but they were so brief that one would have to collect a lifetime of such sounds (essentially Cluster's language was animal jargon) to understand one intelligent thesis.

He began the meeting with a speech. "We must focus on delivering the quarterly quota. We have the chance to show the Grand Box-On-Top, but must quit muddlings and fuddlings, increase synergies, automate ahead, and gather requirements. Yes, let us gather ..." Cluster paused and looked around. He remembered, "...requirements, gather requirements, yes? Yes!" He then followed his speech by various repetitions and combinations of the previous talk. The audience for the discussion would suggest a solution or give feedback at various stages, although this response varied greatly among the group. One fellow would nod vigorously and interrupt with "That is great." Another more nefarious member wore a look of anger and confusion. Then there was dependable old Belinda. She had to fold in her great wings, hooked beak, and keep those talons dulled to not scare her fellow employees (something about talons put fear in the soul). Everything confused her. It was amazing she made it past the incubation labs. It was a wonder she could even recall her name. She interrupted Cluster by asserting, "I am working on everything," which really means she had delegated everything to everyone else.

This type of obfuscation was part and parcel of these types of meetings. No one ever talked clearly or said what they meant, and an intelligent response was often not requested or valued. Instead, what passed for intelligence was gibberish, and again, obfuscation of the type Belinda excelled in. Cluster looked at the crowd and asked, "Questions?" Slippers raised his fin. "Yes, right over here." Slippers asked, "What are the biggest challenges we are expecting this coming year?" Cluster, smiling, responded, "Great question. Belinda, can we answer that?" Belinda was his right leg, right arm or whatever limb he liked her to be.

"Yes, we expect a lot of competition!" Cluster continued to press the room. He looked across at Ari, Joey, Omar, Maureen, Sardeep, Abayomi, Lou. "Any more questions?" The room was silent for a moment. Marty squawked, "Uhm, yeah, what are the biggest challenges?" He was hoping to curry favor and get the same result as Belinda. Cluster, to no credit of his own, had already forgotten that question was asked, but the wrong person had asked it. He snapped, "What do you think?" Joey asked, "How do you view success in the organization?" That set off Cluster. He went off for what seemed a lifetime and concluded with, "Great question Joey." Exhaustion had set in. Everyone tapped out, but the meeting wasn't over yet. The clearing of the throat needed to be conducted. Cluster cleared his throat, then yelling loudly, concluded, "Meeting over."

After the meeting was over, everyone ambled, walked, flew, or crawled back to their desks. Standing around the desks was Ari. With his ruffled ears, sensitive, overly long limbs and wet slicked back hair, Ari had the appearance of having walked out of a double downpour of rain. He was standing outside of the meeting room. He kept meandering back and forth, peering over. He had arrived a few minutes early waiting for the meeting to end with the intent of seeing none other than Cluster. Folks were shuffling out, and there was Cluster! Ari moved over to him, "Cluster! Can I talk to you for a quick minute?" Cluster looked at him, and then at one of his devices. "I have to run, but go ahead. You have 30 seconds."

Cluster liked to give the impression of always being busy. Only a person of status and importance was busy. They ask for a minute, you give 30 seconds: the rule of cutting down employees to cutting down available time only raised the rank of the manager. Corporate physics required it; to go up, someone had to go down. He purposely ran late to some meetings, and of course, chided those who ran late to meetings, ironic justice being a general flare of only the elite managers. He'd schedule meetings because that's what management did. Meetings at some point in history might have actually been for information sharing and creating consensus. Maybe it was something more, but yesterday, today, and tomorrow meetings were a way to remind the employee there was a control structure, with Boxes-On-Top giving employees directives from above. It was a public hanging, flogging, or at best the theatrics of nonsense and the mundane. It was also shown by HR that physical creatures had to be limited. They needed direction; that is what the HR studies found, and who better than HR to understand organic conditioning? Ultimately, for Cluster and other Boxes-On-Top, the more meetings the more demand there was for Boxes-On-Top, whether that demand was real or fake. The increased appearance of engagement led to the increased impressions of social importance. Network, talk, be seen, repeat, complain about being busy, repeat, talk about global projects as if involved, repeat, take pause, and everyone forgets.

Ari had created a potential meeting out of some kind of vague demand. Cluster was getting impatient, stuck in his own thoughts, "Well, get along with it Ari." Ari began complaining about how slow Sardeep was, how incompetent Omar was and so on. He also didn't understand why we were going to use databases. Ari said to Cluster, "Why use databases when we have the files?" Cluster responded, "Why not? Files are ancient technology. Where did you even get those?" Ari persisted, "Well, I just don't know how data folders enabled technologies." It was a rare moment that Cluster was the voice of reason and fact. "You mean databases." Ari's face turned away as he rifled through files, "See, here…and here…see here…also, I want an office." Cluster was getting a bit frustrated, "Uhm, Ari, get to the point." Ari stopped, "Just too much technology Sir! We need to go backward to go forward." Cluster responded, "Uhm, sure, anything else?"

It took a rare breed to cause a manager to want to end a meeting early. Ari clearly enjoyed double-crossing and taking on anything as a complaint. He was vindictive, to say the least. Cluster ended it with, "More research Ari," and began walking away. Ari danced in place and never feigned interest in any specific cause. He was mostly free of ideology. Ari walked back to Cluster, "Well, Cluster, if I may, we do this for the corporation, I mean, that's why we do this right?" Ari had somehow made it far in the corporate structure, all the way up to management, but this was attributed more to his sinister qualities, the chief of which was his capacity for betrayal. He was the grand betrayer, a *betrayor umbrator*, which he tried to conceal under airs of professionalism. He was no thug, had no real physicality or impressive presence, but was actually a rather slimy sort of individual. Most employees avoided him, and his intel wasn't worth much, but he modeled the unspoken accepted role of being a corporate tool, and that gave him some semblance of power. He always had both an open-door policy and a report-on-site policy, in service of the management.

The one-sided suffering caused by Ari's accusations and pestering was different than that of Zach or others. Zach for example was after the individual regardless of reward, promotion or otherwise. He took pleasure in the hunt itself. Ari, on the other hand, wanted the reward of being right and standing apart. His arrogance and ego were so grand, he felt sanctified and secure just being able to gain the audience of a Box-On-Top and registering complaints. He enjoyed watching others fall. While Jake was walking back, he saw Ari walk out with Cluster. He wanted to tell Ari, "You think you're better, deserve better, you fink, you liar?" But instead he thought to himself, *What for? The truth got you nowhere here, it wasn't truth that mattered, it was appearance, presentation, willful blindness.* Jake started analyzing the non-existing benefits of telling Ari what he thought to his face. He thought to himself it would have felt good to have said something, and that is worth it sometimes. Jake could make a mountain of a mole hill (no disrespect to moles), but he always overrode his gut instinct and suppressed his anger. Still, he wondered. Who you are is with you forever, trauma lasts forever, memories seem forever, but you only get one soul. Maybe speaking up saves the soul. Who knows?

Chapter 8:
Training

Everyone queued up, waiting for the meeting room to empty. The previous group of attendees started walking out and around the newly formed queue. The sign over the room read, "*Anti-Harassment Training*." Jake chuckled to Sardeep, "Harassment of who? The employee?" Sardeep looked away as if he didn't hear him, "Uhm, what Jake? Sorry, didn't hear you. And you know this harassment is for everyone." Jake quipped, "Oh, harassment for everyone? You mean harass everyone? Is that the equal opportunity part of it?" Sardeep moved away, and Jake could've goaded him further, but he didn't. Where was HR? Caelestis, Celesete…one of those subservient evil-doers would be here to make sure no liabilities or liberties were taken.

Out of the room and around the corner came out a long elegant double horned beauty. Everyone stared. Magnificent stride, presence, and double horned! She sat down, and everyone followed suit. She started unscrewing her horns. They must have been fakes! Then she opened her mouth and screeched, "Goooddd mornnning everyone!!! I am Ben-Her and Andres will be joining us remotely!" If the evaporation of motivation and desire could be visualized as plumes of smoke, the room would have been filled by now with bad air. That particular combination of shrieking address had finally met its friend, fraudulence. "Poof!" went the enchantment inspired by her beauty, with the potential of the meeting, with the topic. And to top it off, who was Andres? An intra-inter-extra…company transfer? The communication pad sitting on the table lit up. Ben-Her hit the code on the pad and a voice popped on, "Hello all. I am Andres, the consultant." Oh no! The no-good consultant. A master of none and a jack(er) of people's time and energy. Occasionally, they were also useful for deflection, blame, and awful spreadsheet work. Their core offering was inefficiency and overhead, so it made sense that their hiring came directly from the Boxes-On-Top. Absurdly consultants did not even arrive prepared; they had to be trained to do the thing they purportedly sold themselves as capable of doing. They ultimately created more work and strain than they solved for and to save face the only success path for management was to fix the consultants failure through the employee. Suddenly the employee now had to do the work the consultant was hired for, send it back to said consultant and have them label it with their consulting brand to give the image of success.

Consultants would float around and from company to company on loan, retainer, and occasionally on free snacks and swag (but they didn't get the good swag, not the logos on shirts, logos on stickers, logos on logos—they received gifts you would receive that had no real purpose). "So, let me introduce myself. I am Andres, and I work for you, for BLC, for all employees. I'm here to tell you that our goal today is to run a training on harassment, how to identify it, deal with it, and, of course, escalate it." *If there was only an emergency button or eject button*, Jake thought. You'd just pop through the window and parachute out or teleport or evaporate away from this scene of misery. Andres continued, "Ben-Her, did you want to add anything?" Oh boy, did she ever, did anyone ever—there was always someone who wanted to add something, "Yes, yes. We here at BLC Corp put the client, the employee, first. We are here for you. You are here for us, yes, yes."

Sardeep raised one of his many legs, hair prickly, multiple eyes zoned in, "Will we be able to take notes?" *Ah, smooth move*, thought Jake. *This will gain you some points Sardeep.* Ben-Her said in that fake tone, with her loud shrieking booming voice, "Great question, Sardeep. You take notes! Takes notes for us all." Jake elbowed Sardeep and whispered, "You did it to yourself." Sardeep's eight eyes moved around wildly. Andres said, "Jake, sounds like you want to volunteer as well?" Jake thought how the hell did he detect that…that damn consultant. Jake responded, "Yes, yes." Ben-Her, said, "Jake, are you imitating me?" Jake said, "No, no" and snickered. He had better stop before some real infringement took place. Andres, said, "Ok, so what does harassment mean to you Jake?" Jake thought to himself, *What was the most innocuous response*? And replied, "Be nice to everyone. One BLC!" Andres bought it, "Yes, good job, Jake. Ok, and today that is what we are talking about, but more broadly, the importance of recognizing harassment. What is it? Well, it is bullying, plain and simple, based on different approaches. Ok, let's ask—Geraldine, what is bullying?" Geraldine shuffled around in her chair. She was muscular, intelligent, and liked to chew cud from time to time, but she definitely hated bull. Geraldine shoved herself backward in her chair and said, "Uhm, Bullying? Because a Cow would know about bullying? And who told you the males bully us females? They are males, but why would you assume that I would be bullied, and what are you again, Andres?" Andres said, "Uhm, a consultant. Listen, I didn't mean bullying, as in bulls." Ben-Herr started typing rapidly, and Andres on the call switched targets, "I meant…well, let's take this to Sardeep. Thanks Geraldine."

Andres knew Sardeep would be a safer response, "Yes, bullying is not good. One should accept all hoofs, horns, lack of horns, fins, and all of it. One should stand on top of the highest floor and shout equality, freedom and BLC Corp. We have to support each other and respect each other." Andres said "Yes! And what do you we do if there are indiscretions? Indirections. Uhm, Indiscretions!" Everyone was a bit confused, but there seemed to be a point. Andres said it again, "Indiscretions against the employee? What do we do? Uhm, Sardeep?" Twenty-five others in the room and he went to Sardeep. "Yes, sir, we will report to our Box-On-Top and our HR representative," Sardeep replied. "And what will the outcome be?" Andres asked. Jake thought *Keep quiet...just keep quiet.* Billy—good ole Billy would say something, and he did. He said "Discipline!" Andres, said, "Yes." Billy said, "Well let's just say the individual had a few strikes against them. What discipline are we talking about?" Andres' voice quivered over the compad, "Oh Billy—I don't know if we can go into that." Ben-Her started typing again, and Andres quickly stated, "Yes! And we, well, Ben-Her, do I tell them?" Ben-Her said "Yes, yes, get it over with." Andres, flustered, said, "Billy, we verbally—verbally warn them!" Everyone in the room looked confused. Billy said, "So you can repeatedly harass and get off with a verbal warning?" Ben-Her intervened, "Billy, we take verbal warnings seriously."

Jake gave Billy a look, warning him to stop now. *What an eight-layer fake pie of bull*, thought Jake. No one else looked particularly inspired, but the training box was checked off. Next were the other corporate courses and trainings, on securing your system and self, knowing your customer, what wattage was appropriate in a circuit breaker, how to prepare when elevators don't work. Training was a business in itself and started with good intentions, meant to satisfy enhancements to the company and employee, but ultimately ended up a checklist for gratifying the belief that employees were getting some focus. Its real intent was to create a uniform corporate culture and most importantly, to confuse and mystify employees. Jake sent a message to HR Corp:

From: Jake <WolfDog@BLC.divison4.net>
Sent: Thursday, Shaban, 1439, 529039
To: HR Corp <HROverlords@BLC.divison4.net>
Subject: Re: Security course? Is it offered?

"Hi HR Corp,
I am interested in the course on security.
Thanks,
Jake"

Jake thought, *I'm not actually thankful, but dear, hi, hello, thanks, sincerely, all were empty words. Then again, you didn't want to be rude because society tells you not to be rude! And well, society always does what's right by people? Right? Yeah.*

From: HR Corp <HROverlords@BLC.divison4.net>
Sent: Thursday, Shaban, 1439, 341039
To: Jake <WolfDog@BLC.divison4.net>
CC: Cluster
Clust_Er301@BLC.divison4.management.net
Subject: Re: Re: Security course? Is it offered?

"Yes, cc'd Cluster".

Jake thought, *Why would they cc my boss?*

From: Jake <WolfDog@BLC.divison4.net>
Sent: Thursday, Shaban, 1439, 529039

To: HR Corp <HROverlords@BLC.divison4.net>
Subject: Re: Re: Re: Security course? Is it offered?

"It's okay, I withdraw my interest.
     Jake."

Jake thought to himself, *I have to beg to take a course, that benefits the firm?! Ridiculous.*

Email (as it was still affectionately called, although it had moved a few levels beyond its original incarnation) seemed so innocuous, but actually it was a vehicle for a power struggle first and a communication fifth or somewhere later on in reason for usage. Tricks and tactics of the trade were tested and applied against employees in word duels representing amorphous power struggles, but sometimes also between management, employees, HR, departments, and even clients. Management was FYI'ed. Who sent and received e-mails indicated rank and conveyed respect and helped the corporation audit trails and package surprises of disappointment and work orders. It was never just an e-mail. Jake thought *Forget this training.*
       Joey came by, "Jake, what's with the long face?" Jake quipped, "You being smart Joey, or making fun of my snout?" Joey laughed, "No, friend, but just left this security training. Quite interesting." Jake was a bit in disbelief, "Uhm, I've been trying to get that course, but management, HR, just keeps pushing back. I never understand how these decisions are made." Joey said, "Don't worry, you didn't miss much. The usual dodos." Some were brainwashed easier than others. It really didn't take much to brainwash the un-inquisitive, the already-convinced, those who craved validation, and so on. Even Jake had to fight it at times, the desire for validation. He was only a creature after all, like other creatures with the same base desires.

Shame would creep over him every time if he kowtowed (named after Kow, the Cow, who always shamefully acquiesced, pandered, laughed, talked to anyone to be 'part of the group'), or if he wasn't more his natural self. Sometimes you just wanted to be left alone, not smile, be unexcited, not feign interest. But fear and training would kick in, followed by shame washing all over the body and brain, slowly peeling away the conscience like an onion with old folds until everything was exposed.

Jake was ready to walk out, and then he saw the announcement for a birthday party for a few folks next to the digital filing cabinets (digital filing cabinets were everything you imagined. They were, you know, digital, and if you've never imagined digital filing cabinets, you're not dreaming hard enough). A cheap banner and cheaper desserts were set on the tables. A few smiling dolts singing "Happy birthday." Abyoumi was in the center. He was a young pup when they pulled him onto the team. He was fresh out of training, and as Cluster and Tse had said to him, he was a negative value to a company, that his training was payment alone, and that he should be appreciative of the opportunity they were giving him. Abyoumi bought it. That statement of negative value was confounded with learning and could be said about anyone new to a company or business. It was actually a frame of reference and a mental back flip. Really, it was the contrary. You needed the fresh Abyoumis, fertile minds easily absorbing new skills and even more easily breakable. Jake was there once; somehow, with the right connections, he managed to skip the literal breaking point (the point when an employee was ready for programming, after some feedback and training). Whether it was the beginning of the end, or the end of the beginning was irrelevant. If you didn't keep the supply steady with young moldable minds, you wouldn't have senior and more seasoned units of resource, would you? The lab would have loved to replace everyone with robots. Robots felt no pain and were more easily programmable.

Abyoumis' and the young employees would fight over crumbs of work, making even shoveling trash something contestable. When you constrained the supply of work as such, when you elevated the importance of reporting the new IT fix, limited attendance of a boring meeting, picked from a lottery an individual to lead the un-leadable, awarded a nonsense project, or delegated the job of providing the annual update to one person, you created enough infighting and distracted the low-level employees while moving their attention to silly tasks. You made poison that tasted sweet if you were a smart corporation, but you couldn't poison employees too quickly. It had to take its time, and employees had to willingly take it, believing it was anything but. It was Jakes birthday as well, to be celebrated at the digital filing cabinets, but he moved towards the back of the group hoping to go unnoticed. Now, if he could only truly walk away from these constant thoughts, he would have. But he was trapped. He could spend a lifetime worrying, thinking, playing out scenarios and by the time he was done, life would be over. Maybe some lessons learned, but nothing that mattered. Some mistakes weren't necessary or worth the lessons, and the lessons themselves so specialized or painful, he would happily have taken ignorance to the problems to begin with.

To be made an expert in corporate politics and games was a loss bigger than one could imagine. It was a semi-numb, and half-alive state. A corporate zombie of sorts. *A charade of care and a charred bit of cake. Just walk away from the cake,* Jake thought. Neither charade of care nor cake was appealing. Jake was 5 years in, old for his species. He preferred to celebrate alone than with hypocrites and charlatans who would cheapen his day. He saw a few folks rush down the hallway. Hmm, was I missing something? Where was I supposed to be? Oh damn, the standup—Jake was late to the meeting. Heart pulsing, sweat pouring, he started rushing, his excuse generator going full blast, *I was at my desk...I was at another meeting...* Ah, whatever. He showed up two minutes late to the rotation of updates with Boxes-On-Top in observation. A Box-On-Top chimed to Jake, "And what else did you work on?" Maybe the birthday charade didn't look so bad any more.

Chapter 9:
Break Time (Interlude)

Jake hustled in to the break room (not to be confused with HR's break room where…well, we'll leave it at the break room) and looked around for Billy. Sardeep was there. Andi over there. Ok, hmm. Sopaur, shifting on all eight of his legs and dripping ink everywhere with his enormous bubble-like water-filled head, was over in a corner, but Jake wondered where Billy was. They were all gathered there for their lunchtime break. This break was initially granted by HR in collaboration with the Boxes-On-Top when it was observed that employees would 'malfunction' (as organic creatures do, i.e. fall asleep at their desk, make more mistakes, etc.) if made to work too long without a break—after all, they were organic beings, not robots. The fact that HR and Boxes-On-Top needed to see the employees mentally and physically breakdown before realizing they required a break was not so much callousness, as lacking in compassion and a natural result of seeing employees as automatons, as akin to robotic beings not animated flesh. The break for the employee at minimum allowed the belief (real or perceived) that they were disconnecting or getting pause from work and if employees believed something, they would perform marginally better.

In lieu of breaks they were sometimes given trivial freedoms—"Casual Friday!", "Everyone wear jeans on Friday!"—meaning you could dress more comfortably, or "Grab as many snacks as you can hold!"—meaning you could gorge away—although unlike wearing jeans, gorging had a limit (especially if it coincided with jeans that weren't very loose)—unless you were a Sopaur and had eight arms, how many snacks could you hold to begin with? For HR, the Boxes-On-Top, and the lab the robot filled future couldn't arrive soon enough. Although the patent was filed, #920-41-4214-043 and in the works, the anticipation for that future among the management—one without snacks, trivial freedoms, or choices—was high. Employees couldn't wait either. They were told they would not have to work, would get unlimited units to spend, have worlds to explore, and so on. A set of beliefs based on a set of lies based on the disinformation based on…well, basically the employee always was told things would improve. And they would improve—for the management, the owners, and eventually, management would be squeezed out next after the employees. But throwing out the shell of employees and management and keeping the gooey innards for the owners to harvest directly needed super robots. For now, lunch break and general breaks were the easier parts of the workday and easier to implement than these super robots. At any given break time, you could see individual employees wandering around the floors, some headed towards the kitchen or game rooms (balls and things to hit balls with were timeless forms of amusement—games like ping pong and pool provided endless cheap thrills). They used to have a Giant Hamster Wheel in the break room, but only the Hamsters could use that.

Jake walked over to Sopaur. "Hey Sopaur, a game of ping pong? Or chess? Or checkers? Or a video game?" Sopaur laughed, "Video games? Sure chum. What epoch are you living in? Who the hell calls anything video anything. We have holograms, we have all sorts of neat games. We have avatars more realistic than you can imagine." Jake, annoyed, responded,

"And who calls people chum, what do I look like, shark bait? Yeah, sure, so you don't want to play." Sopaur, ignoring him, continued, "What a boring set of options. But ok, let's play. I'm going to win anyway, doesn't matter. Let's make it chess, chum." Jake moved a pawn forward. Sopaur responded with a pawn. Jake snapped a knight from the back row. Sopaur mirrored the move. Jake joked, "Am I playing a mirror?" Sopaur said, "You know chess is an analogy for life?" Sopaur grabbed a chess piece, "See this? This is you." Jake said, "What, a pawn? And what are you?" Sopaur grabbed 8 pawns with all 8 arms, "I am a set of pawns," he said, and snickered.

Jake said, "Well, and who are the knights and rooks and bishops and the queen and king?" Sopaur lowered his voice, "You know who the king and queen are. The rest of the pieces might appear to be rooks compared to the pawns, but it's all relative. They are pawns with copper chain mail and additional clout, but at the end of the day, they are still just tools." Jake responded, "What if someone wants out?" Sopaur said, "Out of what, that cheap suit of yours, Jake?" Jake thought, *Finally! He called me Jake, and I think he just insulted my suit.* "Yes, out of this gig." Sopaur pointed at the board with one of his giant tentacles, "You think there's anywhere past this board chum, you're dreamin', and even if there was what would you do with yourself? What would there be? Enjoy yourself. You take life too seriously." Jake thought. "Well, I guess I do. What other way is there to take life? Lightly." Sopaur delivered the striking blow, and Jake's queen collapsed. Jake was caught off guard, "Wait, how…hold on. Damn—this whole time you're talking my ears off and planning to capture my queen!" Sopaur laughed, "You would have lost anyway. Hey, better on this fake board than in real life." The only thing to console Jake now was food. Jake told Sopaur, "I'm going to get some food."

Jake walked over to one of the kitchen storage units and grabbed the orange looking morsel with white swirls and ingested it. Yuck. What a foul-tasting thing! It looked better than it tasted as he suddenly noticed all the lights went green on his arm pad (it must have been extremely healthy).

Jake looked around again. No sign of Billy yet. They usually tried to take their breaks together. While he was waiting for Billy, he decided to try another item. The granular squares in some sort of polyhedral form. Disgusting. The break room was full of a dizzying array of consumables, silly games, and monitors. In lieu of greater compensation or recognition, one got a bag of colored sugar or salted shapes. The Bureau of HR, Box-On-Top, and the countless other departments would place moles. Conversation there was like conversation in corporations everywhere. Whatever was stated in public was public, and whatever was stated in private was still public. The only thoughts kept secret were those that remained silent and inside one's own head. Even that eventually would be extracted when labs figured out how to detangle brain signals. Or at least HR science hoped to discover such a method. To imagine that future inspired shudders of horror in Jake. The future might hold a workday without breaks but one with more coffee, bags of chips, and the occasional seasonal peanuts (reserved for holidays).

In the middle of his contemplation, Jake looked up and shuddered. Oh no, Eddie and Kevin were walking towards him. Eddie had that dumb, sinister grin that only he could have. He walked heavily, bow legged, and swinging his arms. "Jake, lunch?" he grunted. Kevin echoed, "Lunch? Jake, lunch!" Now why would Jake want to get lunch with Eddie and Kevin? There was no reason to put himself through such torture. Eddie put pretense first. Kevin put his robotic fin suit first. Lunch was a trap. Talk to Eddie and Kevin, and you've just broadcasted to everyone all your secrets. What a couple of clowns. Actually, more like a couple of idiots. Kevin and Eddie yelled in unison "Lunch! JAKE!" Jake just started walking faster in the direction opposite from those two.

He spotted Geraldine! She said, "Hey Jake!" Geraldine could rotate her head all the way around. It was quite a sight. Her lashes recolored so purple that you couldn't miss her. "Geraldine, how are you? Have you seen Billy?" Geraldine laughed, "I see Billy filling up on snacks and talking to you, that's about it, although I did see him chatting with Joey the other day." Geraldine continued, "Jakey, Jake. If you have to think about it too much, you don't know the answer." Jake said, "Uhm, think about what?" Geraldine continued, "There are many flavors to tragedy. Just like the flavors of ice cream here." Poor Geraldine, that's what happens to you when you drink too much of the corporate milk. You start seeing everything in terms of tragedy and ice cream, and you confused your allusions and references.

Jake finally saw Billy and said, "Geraldine! Great catching up. Let's do this again" (by which he meant never), and ran over to Billy saying jokingly, "Billy, it's been ages!" Billy responded, "It's been a few minutes." Billy looked a bit nervous. He looked around. Every time someone entered the room, he'd look back to see who it was, a Box-On-Top or another employee. "Jake, you know there's a life outside of work?" Billy said. Jake responded, "Sure, there is, the apartments and unit." Billy shook his head. "No Jake, there's more in this world." Jake responded with frustration, "This IS the world." Billy paused. Jake repeated, "It's the world Billy. Is your arm control damaged?" Billy paused, still saying nothing. Jake repeated, "Billy, are you okay?" Billy then smiled and said, "Listen, there is a world beyond this. Come to my place after work. I have a gift for you." Jake said, "Bring it here." Billy responded, "No, it's not safe." Jake said "Ok, fine, I'll come by and get it." Billy emphasized,

"You tell NO ONE." Jake joked uncomfortably, "We aren't getting retired to the Department of Lost Souls or Department of the Retired for this, are we?" Billy just smiled and said, "No one will find out. Listen, I'll just bring the gift to you instead" Jake laughed, but he was still uncomfortable. "Uhm, but yeah, so what happens if we get caught?" Billy just winked and motioned his hands pointing toward the back. One of the snitches, Howard, started squirming slowly towards them—but his shell kept him and his trail of slime visible in the distance. This conversation had to end before he arrived (although it might take him forever).

The herds of employees showed up at the right time. Clicks. Clucks. Woofs. The discussions were cathartic, work-oriented, and endless. Time wasting was very much allowed, but only for the right employee. Zach, Sardeep on a good day, Ari, and a few others. Billy and Jake knew they were not the right employees. They both took a path out of the room. They didn't want to be the right employees. That was a sign that they'd lost whatever little identity they had. Normalcy around here wasn't evil per se, as much as it was a degradation of existence. It is normal to love, to hunger, to want, but to want to do a one-on-one, meeting, or be excited about spreadsheets or lunches with Eddie and Kevin—that was when the new normal was dangerous.

Chapter 10:
Back Home

Six days had passed, and the day of rest had arrived! Jake was excited because today, Billy would come over and he would bring a special item, a gift of sorts. Must be a snack box, or maybe a unit wrapped up in wrapping paper. Uhm, yeah snack box. That's easy to gift, or a new program for the arm pad. Ah, guess I just have to wait. The arm pad games he had were getting a bit stale, so a game would be nice. The thing with addictions is they actually never grew old, rather they outlived the user or were replaced with bigger addictions, and occasionally if the user could break away real satisfaction. The user deep down knew this, but hey, that's why it's an addiction. There were a few popular ones, Kandy Krush, Klash of Tribes, Furious Fowls, Re-jeweled, and others that fed the effective compulsion loop, a feedback loop based on pleasure, distraction, and alienation. Every time you played a game, you heard a noise go off and got some digital or synthetic reward.

Jake pulled up his arm pad, and a hologram popped up with a menu of items—

"Welcome back, Jake. Please select your activity."
a). Log work hours
b). Check number of units
c). Emergency 911 (Call in Sick to Work)

d). …Games

Jake tapped on d)… Games, and a new menu popped up.

"Welcome back, Jake."

Jake paused. The device must be broken! Exasperated, he spoke to it, "Yes, yes, you've already welcomed me, games! Take me to games!" Maybe a verbal command would be more expedient.

"Jake, thank you—Games. Please select or search for a game."

Jake started typing into the holographic pad but then decided to just scroll through the list.

a). Kandy Krush
b). Klash of Tribes
c). Furious Fowls
d). Re-jeweled

He selected Klash of Tribes. He was the leader of a massive tribe, and the object of the game was to invade and conquer. After this, you gain rewards and fame as well as other prizes. It was endless. There were enough patterns in the game and enough reinforcement that these micro-loops would hack the organic brain fairly quickly. To be the master of your own destiny (if that destiny was to be the leader of a massive tribe), to have troops to command, to gather resources, to feel in control— the game made you feel powerful. The genius of the game was that it hacked biology. Tens of thousands of years of evolution didn't prepare the organic body for the invention of transistors, games, dumb phones, and more electronic devices. The brain couldn't detect the fraud these devices inflicted upon it, the ways they opened up neurons and triggered real senses and mental constructs. The game did so electronically and made time a blind culprit in its control of the mind. Time, that unquantifiable (despite organic creatures attempting to quantify it with labels of years, months, days etc.), that uncapturable, finite, and most valuable of resources, was exchanged cheaply and transferred into the game, where time was spent. In his speech on corporate welfare, the great Chief Partner of Boxes-On-Top (his special title) at one company famously outlined the game's goal:

> "*God only knows what it's doing to our children's brains...exploiting...social-validation   feedback loop...dopamine...And that means that we need to sort of give you a little dopamine hit every once in a while, because someone liked or commented on a ... or whatever. And that's going to get you to contribute more ... that's going to get you ... more likes and comments...How do we consume as much of your time and conscious attention as possible?*"

It was incomplete gibberish from the historical archive, but the admission and the goals of these electronic devices, games, social networks were clear—to claim your consciousness. The admission was generations too late, and was singular of the millions of messages promoting games; it was too hidden and after these Executives had benefited and before anyone could do anything to stop these addictions. Oh, and there was the hypocrisy of the Executive who managed to send out a message before disappearing. There was also the Executive who did not disappear but who was so high up he could tell anyone to jump off the highest floor and the response would be, "How soon?" or, for the particularly eager...well, they just jumped. Ultimately,

Executives disallowed their own brood from using the products, games, devices, and programs that their own companies produced. Your brood or you yourself didn't matter. But their brood was special. They would be exempt from the brain rot that these devices cultivated. Where was the corporate apology for the loss of focus, loss of time and the mental distractions? From the selling of weapons in the previous eras to the creation of unaffordable medicines to creating these games—corporate history was a history of damage infliction. Well, apology, miscommunication, or confession, or whatever it was the Executive had delivered: rejected.

The amount of knowledge that went into designing these games could have gotten us to distant planets, or cured cancer. The logic was simple: do something, get a reward, have more possibilities. The organic mind sought pleasure in discovery and solving problems. Work gave you worksheets, presentations, robotic arms, forms to fill out, people to go after, but *not* truly discoverable, enjoyable work. Nothing exciting or beneficial.

Wait, Jake thought, *did I just think that?*

Who knows? His brain was fried from all the gaming. He had to put the game down. The modern life was plug in for work, plug in on the day of rest, dream of work, and then repeat. All anyone knew was the modern life. You were bred into it, all senses upon their first entrance to the world knew only that, and there were rumors that even their genes were manipulated, their thoughts injected. Imagine that. The plugs were so integrated at this point that they became extra appendages at times. It seemed more obvious stepping back and looking at it. Why wouldn't something built purely for taking your consciousness and attention do anything but what it was designed to do?

The insipid marketing machinery around it, the unregulated (and regulated-but-lobbied) allowance of such addictive games, devices, and social networking groups didn't help. The trickery of using your peers to convince you, and you to convince them, that this was the quickest way to connect, made employees worse at being alone, and worse at being together. The more obvious thing was to connect someone to a drug directly and induce the dopamine to just get it over with. Stop the charade of independence or choice, or choice only after that choice was prescreened by the corporation and its society. Physical activity was almost entirely absent as was most meaning in life.

Better get a move on, Jake thought to himself.

He got up, fixed his fur, donned his one suit, and disconnected from his feeding tube. There were no public gathering spots; one could only meet others at the office break room or discreetly at their unit. Jake zoomed over to Billy's unit via a tube. His intercom was down. He rapped on Billy's door twice. Billy opened the door with a, "Jake, my friend!" Billy and Jake gave each other a paw-to-hand fist bump. Jake cheerfully started, "So, I've been waiting. Where were you? And more importantly, where's my gift?" Billy said, "Not so fast, friend. Let us talk, but before we do, first, I have some morsels I snuck out for you." "Life is what you make it, Jake," said Billy while handing him these morsels.

Jake was annoyed but continued to eat the morsels, slowly chewing, "Hmm, these are tasty, but back to the point. I waited a long time, Billy." Jake hesitated a little before adding, "And Billy, cut out this 'life is what you make it' stuff. What life? What choices? Clap all your paws upside down, twirl three times, sing 'till you can't anymore, and you still won't make anything change." Billy laughed, "Your remarks are not needed Jake. Shall I continue?" Jake said, "Go ahead!" Billy stared at Jake a bit. Jake started matting his fur a bit, pulling a few hairs out, "Damned grey hairs are wiry." Jake was caught up staring at his grey fur patch. Billy said, "Aging happens to the best of us.

The worst of us too, and when you think of it…all of us, actually." Jake was even more annoyed, "Billy, who said me, why include me?" Billy patted his own matted grey fur, "Look— it happens to all of us, the trick is to enjoy it while we can. Slow down. Stop….and you know what? Be the Silver Wolf you are." Jake started chuckling, "Ok, keep going Billy."

Billy continued, "We have evidence of life on this planet." Jake started laughing, "Billy, I figured that one out. Speed it up, otherwise we'll be completely grey." Billy said, "Our memories are limited, our experiences are limited." Jake interrupted, "And even those that we have are remembered differently." Billy paused, "You sure do interrupt a lot Jake…how about you just listen?" Jake said, "Sorry, got excited, Billy. You're—well, why couldn't other paths exist? Why does fate have to be just work?" Billy started telling Jake stories of roads and four wheeled-vehicles, of communists, socialists, capitalists, fascism, hooliganism, celebritism…that one was interesting. There was worship of the media and celebrities. There were multiple ways to follow them, watch them with their new fashions, find out when they were expecting, see them on their birthdays, on every other day. Celebrity Worship Syndrome (CWS), they called it. Turned out 100% of the population had it to varying degrees. Some people named their kids after celebrities and renamed themselves too (they had extreme CWS), some fell in love with them, and the very extreme cases would look for their trash. Jake thought, *who cared what others wore, and what stupid statements they made? These celebrities sounded mostly like semi-attractive and sometimes unattractive idiots.*

There were stories of blueberries, gooseberries and hulihooberries (it sounded something like that). They came in GMO, GBO, GLO and so on. Apparently, at one point, organic. Most of history people ate organic, but eventually, they started consolidating farms and making more products to generate more profit (Jake knew that one, corporations did that!). The organic created cults, consisting of those who only ate that and those who didn't, Jake wondered if there were wars over this. Talking to Billy, it seemed there were wars for everything until the corporation changed the format for life that is. There were rivers, imagine that, water, running through. What was it, through sand hills or trenches or sides or something? They called them rivers. Creatures were friendlier back then, but apparently even friendliness died before the last few epochs. They would invite each other for meals, call one another, see one another. Then, with the introduction and proliferation of electronic devices, things became textual, flakey, and shallow. There were horrors of rape and murder, ethnic cleansing. *What a dumb and wasteful species*, thought Jake.

Well, at least there was love. Organics (not the food but the creatures) would love each other. Actually, love still existed today, even though it was the most difficult thing in existence. But effort and time were not invested in that. One would lose love for all sorts of reasons: fear of commitment, fear of failure. Jake knew those feelings well. Love that is found easily, apparently is also lost easily. He had his moments. He'd met the right one. He'd let her go. That pain was so deeply buried he didn't like to think about it. This was for another story, too difficult to write now. Jake was enjoying the fantasy that Billy was weaving about history and was also going through some pains hearing it. He had to cut off Billy, "Thanks Billy. Sounds fun, but enough with your stories. Corporations have figured out how to keep society at an absolute minimum. Yes. I *thought* it. You have enough to sedate you. You are busy with the momentum of life. You are exhausted enough that you never think, what else. What next. We are herded and trained *to live only for work*." Billy said, "Just wait, I will get you a gift Jake—you'll see for yourself."

Chapter 11:
The Department of Humane Restriction

HR was always investigating problems ranging from potential breaks in protocol to blasphemy against the Values and Principals. The HR ER was always busy. It was busy with the victims, vagrants, and wanderers; they were coming in from many different departments. This usually happened after a reorg, or some harassment leak, or due to some general misbehavior. The list of offenses to be prosecuted was growing. For example, Offense #142 – two employees caught in the hallway found disrespecting the system by suggesting that work was monotonous – were caught and sent for rehabilitation. Offense # 154 – one employee speaking up (and out of turn) – sent for rehabilitation. Offense #209 – one employee saying "No" on his second offense and due to repeat behavior – sent to the Department of Lost Souls (oh, what an awful department, a place of limbo, retirement, but for those souls that were not to benefit from retirement units, to be sent away in humiliation and worse). Offense #201 – an investigation captured several employees withholding information – three were fined and then sent for rehabilitation. Offense #132 – two employees were caught stealing snacks – sent for rehabilitation. Offense #412 – an employee was appearing combative, exhibiting poor posture and poor attitude – sent for rehabilitation. Offense #341 – employee was late to the office, twice – sent for rehabilitation. Offense

#490 – one employee, caught making up stories of the outside world – sent for retirement.

In addition to meting out punishment, HR also conducted interviews; a new set of transfers were coming in. One of the individuals walked in wearing a clumsy suit. HR began the interview, "We here at BLC prize our employees and believe in work-life balance, compensation, and vacation. You will be meeting with us first, then you will meet some Boxes-On-Top." HR asked its opening question, "Will you please tell us about yourself?" The individual wasted no time in showing his experience, "Yes, I like friends, and work is where you make friends." HR liked naiveté and incompetence in candidates, for only the incompetent could judge it. The candidate droned on, "And snacks and uhm, work." HR took notes, "meets height requirement…mentioned work, yes." HR said, "Yes, well, good—enough about you. Now what about your work history? Tell us about that." The interviewee responded, "Oh sorry, so I started working with data and then started creating reports. We had hundreds of reports." HR asked, "And who used the reports?" The interviewee responded, "Oh, no one." HR responded, "Good, we like to keep things streamlined here. No one is at least centralized and consistent." HR continued, "And what's your five-year plan?" This was a trick question, but the novice interviewee wouldn't know that. The interviewee responded, "I would like to retire early…and…" Before the interviewee could finish his response, HR cut in, "I think we've heard enough." NEXT!

There were numbers attached to each applicant, and someone would pull a number. Number #94 was called and Interviewee #94 walked in, "Hi, I'm excited to be here for the interview for the role within BLC Corp." HR hadn't even given the introduction but liked this candidate's excitement. HR began the interview, "We here at BLC prize our employees and believe in work-life balance, compensation, and vacation. You will be meeting with us first, then you will meet some Boxes-On-Top." HR asked its standard question again, "Will you please tell us about yourself?" The new interviewee began, "I love work, I live for work, work is what drives me. I am passionate about this business, and want to grow with it—I think what we do is critically important." You see what he just did there? He used the royal 'we' cleverly! What 'we' do and threw in 'passionate' as well as other engaged language. HR was salivating, "Ok great, we will send you to the Box-On-Top directly for the next round. But any questions for us?" Candidate #94 thought of every bootlicking question he could. He was a shoe shiner that was for sure. HR sent him along and commented, "That's how you do an interview." The interview was a bit of a joke. It was a special kind of joke, the kind with no ending, no punch line, and that was quite unfunny.

The dialogue and back-and-forth that happened after interviews with HR, Boxes-On-Top and the occasional other employee (those accidently invited to interview candidates to give the appearance that employees select employees) was grim. There was always one foolish Box-On-Top who would argue every employee who was not qualified was and would argue every employee who was qualified was not. There was HR who, in support of that foolish Box-On-Top, would repeat that assessment of the Box-On-Top as if it was their own opinion. There was the less foolish but still misguided Box-On-Top who thought themselves some sort of savior or lord and would purposely overlook or misstate qualifications and bypass the actual interview result. They often let their guilt or need for self-importance be the guide for judging the candidate; they'd make excuses for the candidate, rather than use the metric of hiring. "Maybe they could learn? They are a small group in the representation pool, we need more of this group represented?

83

Maybe, maybe, maybe…." In their litany of excuses on behalf of a candidate, in their overreliance on intangible unquantifiable categories (for example, what was a small group and who defined that?), they often made categorical decisions rather than best hiring practices. Those who felt bad for small groups forgot their historical position of benefit from those very groups. Outward creature features, like fur thickness, ear pointedness, and tail length, were used for centuries to subjugate some species. As if this exploitation of centuries could be reversed through such paltry offerings as hiring practices.

Even more insulting was the queue. The pointedness mattered, and then those with tails would be next, but really insulting was the fact they were queued. HR had all these false and confounding protocols to save face on supporting the employee, when it really resided with the Box-On-Top for the ultimate owner. That was the rub, this same HR department which could not contain any abuse, evil, or harassment would chime in, "Yes, maybe they can learn, we need to represent everyone." The Boxes-On-Top, in their abuse of power, would choose who grew and who didn't, who could learn and who couldn't, and so on. The decision of who to hire was made before any discussion of rational or logical merit took place, this hypocrisy had no bounds. There was even the trained but no less evil and manipulative Box-On-Top looking to harvest the soul of the rare and qualified candidate captured in the ethos. "As long as we can get a year out of them" was the mantra. Life to them was how much they could get out of the employee. The lack of qualified candidates, however, was a grace in itself to the collective soul of employment (if such a thing existed). In a way, if all candidates were capable, imagine the horror in their mass harvesting. Maybe that was the partial justice, that only a few would be burdened and the rest inundated. After the interview and the hiring was the onboarding. One HR representative said to the next, "Hey, you're running late for an on-boarding." The other HR representative responded, "All right, on my way."

What is onboarding, you may ask? Well, on-boarding was another activity done by HR, and shared by the Box-On-Top. Here is one example. The Box-On-Top and HR were sitting together, and the new hire, the former Candidate #94 walked in. The Box-On-Top, said, "Hey, good to see you again! Glad you didn't run away!" The new hire nervously laughed, "Uhm, yes, thanks, nope, this is where I want to be." He'd thought the interview was over. HR started pushing various packets and projected various things, "We'll have some more formal training, but wanted to start you with a bit about BLC history and some of the job rules." HR continued, "When it comes to sick days, unless your pad is disabled or you're dying, you're expected to come in. Avoid any medication that will trouble you at work or surgeries that will delay your return, as this could constitute breach of employment. You are at will. Days off are called the days of rest. Use them wisely. Vacation is discretionary and based on multiple requests to your Box-On-Top. Bathroom use—please limit use and avoid turning the bathrooms into a social club. Get into the bathroom and get out as quickly as possible. Be careful with what you talk about, when you talk, although talk about BLC is encouraged, only the good kind of talk. Any discretion you take should be approved in writing, faxed, scanned, faxed, and re-scanned back to your Box-On-Top and their supervising Box-On-Top including HR. Ok, let me pause. Questions?" The new hire's face had turned a different color, and he stood there breathless and frozen, "Uhm, no." HR said, "Great!" and the Box-On-Top said, "Come, let's go introduce you to the team."

Now the favorite activity of HR and Boxes-On-Top was control, whether it was corralling the sheep, clipping the wings of the birds, telling the monkeys to quit monkeying around, and so on. They generally put a damper on any signs of life or enthusiasm. If you raised your head too high, it would get clipped unless your neck is just too long, but then there were other punishments for you. One could say they were evil, or stupid, or both. One might try to argue an evil HR was worse than a stupid or incompetent HR, but they really all fed the same function and mapped to the same result: pain for the employee. There was one recent scene exemplifying the heavy handedness in public, where an insensitive Box-On-Top was harassing his employees in an induction meeting, "You damn monkeys, always monkeying around!" One employee said, "But sir, what if we are…" The Box-On-Top said, "Do we need to bring HR into this?" And of course, the conversation halted. The Box-On-Top continued, "I should have hired a more loyal species."

In another room, the underwhelming and ditzy HR person showed up at the desk of an employee. Fear spread, public embarrassment ensued, and he was taken to task. He was surprised with transcripts, evidence, and a copy of Principals and Values. He didn't need to hear the rumor. He was the target. He was asked "guilty or innocent?" The judgment was always guilty regardless of his response. It was over. He kept quiet. Clariese began the verbal prodding "Well, you are in trouble, aren't you?" She was flipping through the manual. It says here "Take care for." He corrected her, "You mean take care of…" She snapped at him, "I know what I'm doing." He didn't know if a response was being asked for, so he stayed silent. Clariese continued, "You are in trouble." He said, "Yes, by your rules, I am." Clariese looked angered. "And what other rules would you have us follow?" He responded sarcastically, twisting one of the Principal and Values, "No, rules are the rules, unless they are changed."

Clariese continued, "So leaving your apartment is now okay?" He said, "Sure, we give the corporation everything. What

I did, I did on my day of rest." Clariese said, "We treat you very well, and there's a long line of people who would take this job, yet you show us no respect." He said, "Yeah, everyone would." Clariese was angry. "You went outside of your unit, and you were neither in your unit nor the corporation, so where else did you go?" He knew everything was being recorded. Judge and jury. Clariese yelled, "You KNOW what you did! If it wasn't for all the years you've been here and the ruckus this would make...you are lucky we are only retiring you! You have two weeks, and one more thing, no breaks, no talking to anyone. We're helping you out here," and then she hit a button. Two muscular, short-nosed and pointed-eared fellows walked in, grabbed him, and dragged him away. Only one paper was left at the desk. Orders for the "Department of Retirement."

Word had leaked out about the incident; some unnamed soul was marched towards the HR tank. Jake was listening to Locum, who had a green coat and long legs, and was detailing what he'd seen, "He was asked by Clariese. Clariese from the head office." Jake said "Which Clariese? Was it the one with the grey coat and domed head?" Locum continued, "Yeah, the one who used to work in communications, delivering messages, she took her away." Jake said, "wait, was it 'her' or 'him?' What did they look like?" Locum said, "Yes, he was taken." Jake was confused, "Wait, he or she?" Thoughts started racing through his head of who it could be. Anytime HR came by to your desk or someone was taken away, his mind would race through a list of all his friends. Locum seemed confused. Jake asked him, "Did you see who it was?" Locum said, "Look, I'm trying to tell you..." Jake waited then said again, "Did you see who it was. Who was taken?" Locum said, "No, I couldn't see who was marched into the room." Jake thought, *useless*. He could use the internal messaging system to ask around but that was monitored too.

Chapter 12:
Break Time (A Final Hurrah)

Jake wandered around the halls, not sure what destination to pick, and he ended up in the break room. There was Jimbo. *Quack. Quck. Qu.* Jake interrupted the muttering. "What are you up to Qua- Jimbo?" Jake said, almost slipping and calling him by his muttering. Jake saw an empty cartridge next to Jimbo with some green muck coming out of it. Jake said, "What are you ingesting there?" Jimbo responded, "Some of this green..." Jake cut him off, "Muck? What is that? Looks like seaweed?" Jimbo tried again, "It is a..." Jake interrupted again, "smells like seaweed...hmm, no kale, is it kale?" Who knows what this food would taste like anyway but that's what the text scrolled on the ingesting tubes indicated. Jake told Quack, "You ever wonder why it's free?" Jimbo's eyes lit up, "What's free?" Jake responded, "You know—these snacks." Jimbo said "Because it's free Jake, why does everything have to have a reason?" Jake waited for that response and said, "Maybe they are testing something on us. Maybe it's just for productivity. Maybe." Jimbo cut him off, "Enough of that cynicism Jake. Maybe they just want to treat us, reward us and so what if it makes us more productive?" Jake said, "Well, I'll tell you this, if there's no price to be paid, then guess what YOU'RE the product or service." Maybe they have nano devices embedded, collecting data. *Who knows*, Jake thought to himself. Quak-Jimbo was a special one, but he might have been on to something. Whatever. Jake moved on.

He saw some workers hauling in a booth-like station into the corners of the break room, getting it ready for testing on some unwilling volunteers. Must have found its inspiration via a Box-On-Top invention and made its way into the lab, finally being released for testing on employees, and the odd thing was that it looked like it could fit anywhere: portable, a mini-office of sorts. Jake walked by a few times, visually scanning the small collection of letters on the side, trying to glean something till finally he pieced the letters together: "Home Office," it read. What was that? That would make sense, achieve productivity at every turn by making the home into an office! He chuckled, didn't need to strain to read the label to recognize portable home productivity, just assume anything from the lab is for productivity. The station had various lights, made some chirps and looked like it would fit into an actual unit. Curious. Eddie was sitting in one of them. It looked like it was interfacing Eddie with some digital circuitry. He had a malleable tube slipped into his ears, virtual glasses swung over his eye, and some plugs into his arm pad. What could Eddie be doing there? He sat there for about 20 minutes and then came out. Jake really didn't want to engage but curiosity got the best of him, "Eddie, before you start talking. What was that device?" Eddie smiled, "Oh wouldn't you like to know Jake? This is going to replace you!" Jake laughed, "Ok, Eddie, what is the device?" Jake knew Eddie too well, "It's a WFH Enabler." Jake responded, "WFH?" Eddie replied, "WFH: work from home. We can start engaging the corporation even better from the comfort of home!" Jake said, "And you want that?" Eddie stopped—as if he hadn't thought about it, "Well, I mean hmm…why not?" Jake thought *'Why not,' why even talk to Eddie?* Jake responded, "Forget it," and started walking away.

Eddie still looked like he was thinking, "Ok, come back Jake. It's something about being able to work from home. It actually simulates the office while you're in the unit." Jake wasn't even going to bother responding, but finally he said, "Go ahead and give your day of rest away, Eddie, but I need it!" Eddie still looked confused. The machine in the background was churning out employees, producing a "ping" sound akin to the beep of some kitchen aid. It was odd to see Eddie without Kevin. Oh, there was Kevin. God, was Kevin in one of those machines too? Yes, he was exiting! Jake said, "Kevin, you too. What are you doing?" Kevin replied, "Oh it's a simulator. I was traveling the world." Jake begrudgingly asked Kevin, "So how was it?" Kevin looked half asleep. He had a half smile on his face. He responded dizzily, "You know how metal and pleasure feel combined?' Jake said, "No, and I don't think I would want to."

Eddie continued, "One could reach the ends of the earth in this virtual world, experiencing various fantasies, and ultimately, never have moved physically *at all*. I've always had the sense that things in the real world were false, anyway. Ultimately, though, the barrier between what is real and what is fake is blurry. One could hardly detect the difference." Jake was amazed by how intelligent and articulate Kevin sounded, not to mention how self-aware. It sounded like someone had switched his brain out. Kevin laughingly said, "But look, you gotta follow protocol Jake, and we all know that you're no good at that." With that petty comment, Kevin was back to himself in an instant. To use the same technology for both work and leisure, to create new worlds in which the employee would lose themselves at work, and to create a space for work from home, not only did this blur the lines between what was real and what was fantasy, but it also spoke to an erosion of real life. Soon there would be no life outside of work, and no home, even at home. The lab could always be counted on to create some crazy new invention or suggest some perverse strategy to make employees more subservient or efficient.

In the midst of these musings, Sopaur strolled by Jake. He asked, "Where you trying to go Jake?" To which Jake responded, "Far from you and these two wing bats." Sopaur sloshed through, "Want my advice? Don't let these 20 years at BRC fool you. I'm vested, I'm well liked, I'm someone you should know." Jake laughed, "I should know that you will get me in trouble." Sopaur continued, "The corporation is for the people, or else the people are in the way of the corporation." Jake wanted to throw up, "Didn't know you live by the commandments, Sopaur? Although that does sound a bit off. You sure you memorized that correctly?" Sopaur responded, "Oh, I only know them when I need them, but that's enough to keep those Boxes-On-Top and HR off my back." Jake responded, "I'm surprised at your candor Sopaur." Sopaur replied, "If you want to last Jake, quit rocking the boat. Zach is watching you and others, and why do you always aggravate Cluster?" Jake thought to himself, *How does he know all this*? Sopaur continued, "You want to last 20 years, right?" Jake responded, "Twenty years of what existence?"

Sopaur squeezed towards Jake, "A good life, just accept it. Get to those spreadsheets, enjoy it, learn to live it!!" he screeched. Jake scoffed, "Live spreadsheets! What a joyous life!" he snarled. Sopaur responded, "There's worse out there. You know some people drive for work without sleep for hours and hours. There's some that stand guard, there's some that mine and scrub data." Jake said, "Yeah, I do some scrubbing myself." Sopaur paused, "Oh you do? Well some scrubbing doesn't matter anyway. Actually, they give scrubbing to some of the better employees." Jake said, "Wait, didn't you just say....?" Sopaur interrupted, "What I was trying to say...what I wanted to give you, was feedback, Jake. This is what we are doing now.

I'm giving you feedback, some things for you to work on, obsess with, as you will." Jake thought, *great, this isn't even my manager, and now I'm getting a lecture from an inebriated peon? Does he actually work for management? Whose team is he on, anyway?* Jake felt like a fly caught in Sopaur's web.

Jake hated all these mental gymnastics, but he had to participate. He was forced to balance, whether he wanted to or not. Jake said, "So Sopaur, why is it that when you are more competent you get punished with more work? You get the worse partners and clients? You work more? And I only have to do it for 20 years. Sopaur, I'm not the favorite, and I never will be." Sopaur said, "Well, what if I could help?" Jake wasn't going to fall for it. He'd already said too much. He had to mask any true feelings for survival, and frankly, who knew what Sopaur could or couldn't do. "Listen, Sopaur, I like Cluster, Zach, the team, you—Sopaur. I don't think any rumors running around are true. I'm here for the corporation, and more so, I live its values and want more work." Sopaur moved all his legs together in a clasping motion, "So be it Jake. You will be judged and sentenced. The trial will be held eventually, but your verdict has already been decided." Jake thought, *Great, now Sopaur speaks as if he sees the future and these trials didn't even happen.*

Jake looked around for Billy. There were only a handful of people he wanted to see, and he'd seen the ones he didn't want to see. Where was Billy anyway? He couldn't keep waiting.

Chapter 13:
The Department of Lost Souls

Billy was thinking, *what a sad fate this is for* me. He was told he would be entering Retirement, *not* the Department of Lost Souls. This must be a mistake. Waiting outside of the Department of Lost Souls he kept looking at his flickering arm pad. *How long would this take? The verdict was handed down already, why this charade and mockery? Was there more? Where they going to take his two weeks away too? Were Jake and Geraldine in trouble? Could this be reversed?* What a sad fate, indeed. Maybe being made to wait in and of itself was just the beginning of all of this punishment, to suffer loss of time multiplied by anxieties and compounded by a layering of somatic stress. His anxiety could have taken a pause when he noticed two short-nosed, pointed-ear fellows walking Stermine out of the main doors. They didn't even bother to look at Billy. *What a bunch of zombies,* he thought. Stermine hadn't even looked his way. Billy and Stermine might not have been friends, but there was something to their daily interaction.

Stermine always acted the part of tough guy, pretended that he was as tough as nanocarbon merged with titanium rocks. His philosophy was women and children last, the weak came last, and even the strong were challenged—his motto: 'no prisoners, no pigeons.' From his foreboding, muscular, scaled body to his devastatingly quick tongue, Stermine had parried with many individuals, swept his tail and death followed. He snapped at whatever he wanted and intimidated anyone he could. Stermine wasn't one to play the part of the victim. Now, he looked broken. Tail bent, head hanging down. He looked physically whole—no scars and no signs of physical attack, but there was something missing. What did they do to him? He was just exiting the HR main office, not some fighter's cage? Stermine was breathing at a shallow pace, holding a folder. Billy thought, *What is in that damn folder?* Billy was next. Joey walked out at the same moment looking shaken. Billy tried talking to him, "Joey, what happened? You see Stermine?" Joey said, "I'm sorry Billy. Stermine…" and then he was prodded away by the short-nosed, pointed-ear fellows. Billy thought, *they got Joey, Stermine…*

Caelestis, a seeming clone of Celeste, walked out of the Department of Lost Souls and called Billy in. Wait. No, someone else—of course, more wait. Caelestis said, "Wait, not your turn yet Billy, next!!" Two more hours passed, *damn it. More time to think.* Amazing how courage and anxiety start mixing. Billy thought of a story that was often told to the employee, a story spread most likely by either HR or Boxes-On-Top:

> *There was the Employee who cried Wolf. He would show up and outright lie to HR and his Box-On-Top. He'd claim he was sick. This young, naïve, and fuzzy-eared employee would get bored with his work, and start itching for more, both literally because of all the darn bugs, and because he wanted more. Not more work. Just more fun, and free time. What a greedy and unwise employee. He cried out to his fellow employees that his work is done and that a Wolf has come by to give him more work. Doubling down! He claims the work is done*

and crows to all his fellow employees this grand news and they praise him.

To his knowledge, there is no wolf, yet, but here was this employee who cried Wolf! He was skipping work, leaving early, coming late and enjoying his days. In all actuality, there was a wolf, and this Wolf with a capital W would show up to reckon for this wayward rooster, with a lower-case r. Apparently this kept happening over and over, until at some point the Wolf actually arrived. Lo and behold, the Wolf howled, scowled, and handed out work assignments. He huffed, puffed, and blew away the employee's cover. What did the employee expect to happen? He was caught, and the employee had to do more work! At this point, he was so behind, due to his own disastrous crying and lying that he didn't get any work done and the work had piled up on him! The Wolf of course had to write up the employee, and, then...possibly gobble him up.

"What a charming story," scoffed Billy. The moral was don't say you're busy and take more work, and don't exaggerate how busy you are. That or don't use the same lie twice. Otherwise you will be detected. Or maybe it was "lie to the right person" or "build a lie within a lie." *Who knows, and who cares?* Maybe this was one of those times where lying would be an honorable effort. Finally, he was called in. Caelestis wasted no time and immediately started to explain the system, "Billy, Clariese told me everything. We sell pain wholesale. What seems to be a prison is a heaven. We make processes, even the process of lost souls, efficient. Is there not a beauty in that?" Billy, knowing it was over, responded, "Sure, in an insane sort of way—but I have to ask, I thought I was going to be retired?"

Caelestis finally feeling some agreement responded, "Yes, now you understand a bit more Billy and yes, we did originally plan on retiring you, but really you might spread knowledge of the outside world. This world does not exist." Billy, not wanting to give away one of the only things left to him—his dignity and a mind he'd struggled to free—responded, "I said in an insane sort of way. Everything done insanely can be argued to be sane."

Caelestis continued, not picking up the subtlety, "Billy, you know what you did, correct?" Billy responded, "Surely, being free, freeing my mind, and breaking the rules were my crimes." Caelestis responded, "Don't be dramatic, Billy. You wandered off and we have various sources that tell us you have artifacts you shouldn't have. You want to tell us what you have?" Billy was caught grey-handed, but thought to test what they knew. He responded, "You mean the tea bags I took from the office?" Caelestis ruffled through her notes, "There was no mention of this...you took tea bags Billy!" She was outraged. Billy thought, ok, if she is this mad about tea bags, imagine how mad they would be to find out what he really took. He might have had no choice but to escape discovery via feigning foolishness. Billy said, "What if I admitted breaking the rules?" Caelestis eyes opened up, "You'll admit it Billy?" Billy smirked, "Admit what?" *What was the point? It was over, and his condemnation was decided before he'd entered the office.*

The ancestors before had allowed the rise of corporations to this level. They were fiefdoms with lords, and no samuaria...samurai...wait, samurai as the stories of knowledge he'd found before had stated. How could they have foreshadowed this future? Well, pretty easily. Caelestis cut off his thoughts, "You just admitted to breaking the rules. Now, we've searched your place Billy. We couldn't find anything, but we know you're hiding something and that you've done something. We are all-knowing and will find out." Billy said,

"Can you predict what will happen 5 minutes from now? What about 15 hours, or 2 weeks? You can't predict past your long nose." Caelestis said, "We are doing you a favor, despite, what you've done to us." Billy had to say something, "What have I done to you? Said no? No, not even that…I've taken some time back. Time is not contained in your databases, your sheets, your construction materials, your coffers. Show me if you are masters of time." Caelestis responded, "Ridiculous—of course we can't move you through time." Caelestis took a breath, and continued, "And Billy, what do we do here?" Billy was confused, "Yes?" Caelestis repeated, "What do we do here?" Billy was getting tired, "We sell products, provide services. We…uhm." Caelestis responded, "Yes, and we move products and services, not time, Billy. Don't make us responsible for your choices. If *we* didn't do it, someone else would. We are catalysts of progress, of speed and innovation." Billy tried to respond, "I've learned, and know more." He paused, "I can tell you we would have gotten there, we, all of us, without having to have made a deal with evil and sacrificed our souls." Caelestis responded, "You exaggerate." Billy responded, "The point is we could have made the medicines, the inventions, the products, all of it, in a better way, without destroying part of ourselves." Caelestis responded, "Are you done?"

Billy was going to continue and Caelestis interrupted, "Maybe we will be magnanimous and retire you. Maybe we continue you to the department of lost souls. But your time is over and certainly we will be your arbiter. Don't concern yourself" Billy's face drooped. He knew it was coming but couldn't figure out how'd he actually act. He wanted to feel strong and brave, but he just felt tired. Billy must have been followed near his building when he went to… but how? He had spoofed his tracking pad. His mind was in a muddle. How did they find him? Could he have prevented this? He knew Caelestis was watching him. It was over, but if he could limit the pain and not drag Jake into it, then he would. Caelestis said, "Anything you want to tell us? Anything Billy?" She paused. Caelestis said, "Let us know how you want to end this. You will be allowed back to your desk and apartment one last time to gather any remaining items." Billy knew the latter was just them following him—his apartment had already been inspected. How would everyone take this? When would this action be discovered by the others? Hopefully at least Jake and Geraldine and the few good creatures were safe.

Chapter 14:
WURK

"Wurk, wurk, wurk..." positive Jimmy was crooning happily. "Wurking the day away!" Jake walked by. "Jimmy, what are you working on?" Jimmy exclaimed, "I'm changing the world!!!!" Jake responded with, "Yeah?" Jimmy replied, "I'm wurking on challenging problems and usaging." Jake was flummoxed. He asked, "What is usaging?" Jimmy replied, "Yeah, utilizing...that's what I meant." Jimmy continued, "I'm implementing the action items so that we can transition them over." Jake had to cut him off, "Listen, is this code for something? I still don't know what you mean. Plain language, what are you working on? Before we have to get a corporate translator in the room." Jimmy looked a bit paranoid now. "Jake, you know...it's hard, it's hard." Jake was confused, "What?" he barked. Jimmy was cowed. He responded slowly, "Ok, you want to see what I'm really working on?" Jake, peered around cautiously, "Sure?" Jimmy minimized the screens. "Let me close this. Won't need this project timeline. Hold on, let me move this column   here,   data   goes here...metadata...taxonomy...ontology...psychology." Jake said "That's fine, Jimmy, were you actually going to show me something? Enough with the ology's: psychology this, ontology that..." Jimmy was a talker, and Jake was a talker, so to hear Jimmy talk was quite the experience until his words began to run together. There were few Jimmys in the world. Whether he was foolish or intelligent, he was at least sincere.

Jimmy kept talking, "So they were telling us in training that we are fortunate enough to be here because if the corporation didn't take the risk, the founders, the originals, I mean, we wouldn't be here now Jake, so we are lucky they gave us a job." Jake responded impatiently, "Are you done?" Jimmy said, "No, and well, we are replaceable." Jimmy looked sad. Jake said, "Replaceable? No, my friend. Well, ok, yes, we are, but so are they, no? Do they ever mention that *they* are replaceable? No—but you are. Just agree we are all replaceable, but it's a 'we' when there's work, and a 'they' when the profits roll in. Jimmy responded, "Ok, but we are replaceable. They made the company. That's a fact Jake. That's a fact." Jake said, "If you keep repeating it, you'll believe it. There were some things that seemed nice, you know, reliable – small checks with units, no risk, a belief that you had no responsibility, no risk, now you gave it up to a small entity. We were born into the society." Jimmy responded, "Look whatever you want to call it."

Jake was afraid and angry. Neither of these feelings was a good feeling. It was a chronic pain just like that damn backache: dull, and always around. All this seemed to be some rubbish, but Jimmy did believe it. You didn't know where things were going or coming from with Jimmy, but you knew he believed them. He was exercising that naïve sincerity again. Jake said, "Well hey, Jimmy, so what is it that you wanted to show me again?" Jimmy yelped, "Here it is!" Jake took a look and it was a mash of colors against a mash of lines on a mash of some other surface. Trying to discern this was going to take some work. The only thing that Jake could tell was that this was art and was creative. What he couldn't figure out was which department could have possibly asked for this.

Jake asked Jimmy directly, "Jimmy, is this art?" Jimmy looked around, "Can't say Jake, but what do you think?" Jake said, "Well *if* it was art, I would say overall, creative, vibrant, colorful, but who am I to say Jimmy?" *Was that a person flying in the image? Or wait...that was a fish...or space ship...uhm...better ask.* Jake asked, "Jimmy what is it to you? Let's say it's not art, but if it was, what is it?" Jimmy responded, "It's my imagination." Jake started laughing. Jimmy said, "What are you laughing at?!" Jake responded teasingly, "Jimmy, Jimmy, where are the deliverables?" Jimmy didn't understand the sarcasm, "But these are charts, reports—I mean, this busywork and bureaucracy are unnecessary! I'm sorry, I know I shouldn't have." Jake said, "I'm giving you a hard time, Jimmy." Jake was amazed at Jimmy's' views. "Jimmy..." he tried to interrupt him. Jimmy kept going, "We report this out, update that, send this to the Boxes-On-Top, metrics for this, metrics for that, metrics for metrics...this is, this is...just wurk."

Jimmy, looking apprehensive, asked Jake, "You ever scared Jake? Jake was confused, "Sure, perhaps. It depends. Not sure if it's from anything real, but why do you ask?" Jimmy said, "Well, I mean have you ever been scared, that even if you dream, even if you wish, and hope instead of try and do, that it doesn't make a difference? Look where we are now, and tomorrow looks like it would look like today. This work and *all* work is pointless. As much point as there is in my own snout," and he started laughing. Jake laughed a bit as well. Jake said, "Listen, my friend, keep doing your art, don't show anyone, we might not have control, *but* we have to imagine we have more control than we do, and we have to try to believe in something else. Or in something else that has meaning, and if that's art for you, then so be it."

Jake wasn't sure he believed himself at times. He just responded with what sounded good, but who didn't have doubts?

Outside of those vested Boxes-On-Tops and the Owners, it seemed everyone had doubts. One of the few good deeds that could take place in a corporation was supporting and comforting a friend. Jimmy asked, "What happens next Jake?" Jake stopped, "Well, you breathe in, you breathe out, you walk forward, sometimes back, but you keep going. The organic creature's ability to predict accurately is quite awful. Everyone almost always misjudges situations terribly. They can imagine so many permutations that don't occur. They take fears and extend them into realities—though sometimes they do become realities." Jimmy said, "What?" Jake said, "Look everyone gets it wrong." Imagining disaster once felt too often; doing it twice felt endless. He didn't want to think about this anymore, so he said goodbye and got up to leave.

Jake started walking towards Andy. He walked in on Andy moving his antennas around, feeling for any electromagnetic waves nearby. His black coat glimmered and his wings were sheathed. Andy looked out and asked, "Jake, are you there?" Jake was right in front of Andy!!! Although Andy was not known for his visual acuity, his antennas had detected Jake. Andy continued, "Hey Jake—can I bring down the temperature a bit? The room's a bit cold—you have that thick coat—I just have my thin shell." Jake said, "You and everyone else is always cold, but just a few degrees up on the thermometer will kill me!" The struggle over room temperature began. Employees weren't solicited much for their input, not into their career, their work or their future, but dammit they had control over the temperature!! Each began to dig his own trench. Andy said, "I know Jane has a cough—and this temperature is too cold….and….." Jake gave up. "Sure. Andy, just leave the temperature where it's at." Andy responded, trying to be conciliatory, "Jake, you take things too seriously!" to which Jake replied, "Well, serious things are serious, and life is serious." With that final parting shot, he got up to leave. It was too cold in there.

In thinking about serious things, Jake began to muse on the nature of what he was doing here and why was he at work. *What kinds of thing do we even produce at work?* He thought to himself. *We make things for consumption. Because, well, creatures exist and that's how things survive,* thought Jake, *by working and consuming.* The equation was something like this: work + oxygen + water = life. If Billy had been around, they could talk this through. The nature of their work and its meaning was something he and Billy debated often. Jake had the kind of job that was considered white collar. There were some that they called blue collar and some that were brown collar. The color of your collar or the designation of your work was directly associated with the type of work you did. Hence there is no need to explain what brown collar was associated with—literally the most basic and most dirty task there is: cleaning of all the defecation produced by all these organic beings. It didn't signify chocolate, that's for sure. Work could even take something like chocolate, which tastes great, and make it bitter, for those who have to produce it, harvest it, bake it, cook it, and never get to touch it, much less consume it. It is just a brown load of excrement the brown collar workers had to remove.

One thing brown collar workers had going for them was that they at least worked with substances directly rather than pretend to work with substances or manufactured false substances or 'services' (i.e. set up a meeting, make another call, make a different call about the meeting). Jake pulled up to his desk and put on his virtual gloves—it was time to get to 'fixing.' He spoke into the arm pad and issued a command, "Status of Open Tickets." The machine responded, "304 open tickets, 245,491 tasks, 495,542…" Jake interrupted, "Stop, just open tickets due this month. Or the most recent request." The machine started sorting through the message, back and forth, cutting through the wave of spam email, HR reminders, Box-On-Top check-ins, colleagues trying to pawn off work, and finally found an actual client request:

> "**From:**   49209-Client-Encrypted@hl.caff.33.##.172.52..542…
> **To:**   ServiceDrone-BLC-424@fla.cda.11.##.192.42..441"
> *Dear BLC – we are requesting a transfer of 15 customized and collapsed tubes declogged and shined ASAP per order # 5299042-4252401-31-34134.*
> *Regards,*
> *Juanguacto*"

Jake started moving the arms through the pathways to dig through the recycled areas for material parts. He quickly gathered a few items and threw them in the de-cycler. He pulled his hands out of the gloves to start running various scenarios, and then entered the numbers into a separate sheet. The de-cycler made quick work of the materials and stated '12.5% carbon required, 3.2% copper.' Jake would then feed it into the multi-dimensional printer and send it to packaging and shipping. Although it was pretty rare, there was a slim amount of satisfaction in completing a task or seeing a task to completion. It was not often that Jake was responsible for useful product creation. He couldn't figure out what 15 specially made water coolers emblazoned with glow-in-the-dark plugs would be used for, but hey, 'people needed what they wanted!' as the slogans of old said. Or was the slogan 'make it and they shall come?' It was all getting jumbled in his head, but it was impromptu break time. Or time for break time?

Jake looked around for someone to engage in conversation. Spotting Sowel, he said, "Sowel, how are you, it's been a while." Sowel said, "You on break?" Jake laughed, "Attempting to create a break, shhh!" Jake looked around for any Box-On-Top and continued, "So what are you having a good time with Sowel?" Sowel shook her head in various directions. She moved her horns, fluttered her big ears, and shuffled her large limbs, extending her long snout in the direction of the monitors. "I'm generating reports and updates, reporting on the new financials, new metrics, analytics...you know stuff that tells you what you're looking at cross-sectional and in a time-series fashion to make decisions." Jake laughed, "You mean indecision? When was the last time we actually shifted goals based on real data and real analysis?" Sowel looked confused. She responded slowly, "Jake, why do you like to make trouble? You know how things work, so just leave them." After that admonition he bid her farewell and walked away.

On his way out, Cluster called him over, "We have a meeting!" he boomed. *It never ended.* How did Cluster seem to always know where Jake was? Cluster said in a calm voice, "Hey, we got some feedback from a customer and partner that we'd like to review with the team." The room was full of staff. Cluster began, "We have a customer emergency. We have gotten a complaint and need to discuss a plan on how to resolve it. Let's review first."

Purchased a used vehicle here 4203, Adzam 6 SuperSporty

Communication/ Review

Gripe #1: How many times do you have to call this place to hear "Can we put you on hold..." or being transferred (and no one picks up...)—they are quick to accept payment...and that's about it, if you gave them pagers/faxes/satellites, they still will claim 'we did not receive that call'...oh, sorry, didn't realize you don't own answering machines, and phones don't record who called them these days."

Management / Review

Gripe #2: The 'bragging about his young mate and complaining about his ex-mate, uhm, ok, relax, don't crud on your staff or me as your customer any more. Please just respond to the question/complete the service you offered/deliver the merchandise etc...no, I don't feel bad for you because you're a millionaire...me, and your staff are victims."

Service center / Review

Gripe #3: Service center...by the time they see you, the Apocalypse will arrive (and that's IF you made an appointment...which is a foreign concept). This is a classic conundrum...how does one fix their vehicle, if they never SEE you...it starts the endless loop

I could keep going.

Staff / review

Sorry ~~Employee 1, Box-On-Top, Employee 2~~, that you work here...

Cluster continued, "Any ideas on how to resolve?" Jake said, "Turn off the complaint box and discontinue customer feedback?" Everyone laughed. Cluster said, "Jake not now...Eddie, Kevin, what do you think?" Jake thought, *great, ask those two morons.* Eddie and Kevin looked at each other, and responded in unison, "let us ask Sardeep...Sardeep, what do you think?" Sardeep, elated he was chosen, said, "Well, what do I think?" Eddie and Kevin smiled at each other, "Hurry it up Sardeep!" It was always funny how those two would somehow sync up in their timing of abuse. Sardeep, said, "Well, can we give them a few units?" Cluster laughed, "Give units...ok we've heard enough." Cluster said, "Jimmy, come over here...call them, and walk them through our process, and try to send them a few parts to fix. If that doesn't work, keep working through it till we have to send them a new vehicle. Jimmy had no choice. "Yes, yes, will do, will do." Cluster patted himself on the back, "Good job team, everyone can go now." Jake thought, what was the point of a meeting if Jimmy was going to be assigned a difficult customer? How was this a team effort? The idea made him cringe. The idea of a team was bankrupt.

Chapter 15:
De-Automation

Jake walked around looking for Billy. Where was he? He ended up walking by one of the labs where some strategic automation work was taking place. Automation, of course, meant things would work by themselves with no direct creature intervention, and that meant the owner had absolute control, so....well, the ultimate owner dream of control—the ability to remove the body of the employee, with all its friction and impenetrability, and replace it with a thing that you could directly command and imbue with your will. This thing could be a creature of maximum efficiency at work. No more bathroom breaks, no more 'sick days' and less work, no more need for swag and rewards and even emails. This new automated thing would be a creature of pure commands. Never could it spew 'no' from its hard drive, only extreme 'yesses and 'processing completes.'

Automation was drummed up and pummeled into the mindset of all teams, projects and groups. The propaganda marketed to the employee was that if automation was 100% percent complete, it would ultimately 'free' the employee to be as creative as possible. This creative creature was mostly a myth, however. The ownership of freedom, or truth could never be copyrighted, inscribed into legal documents or attached to a price—but that didn't stop the corporation from trying. The truth really was that it was impossible to fully automate. You were trying to automate an organic world, that had organic needs and organically driven processes, that were by their very nature unnatural to a machine, a world that naturally had error terms and chaos built into it, and logic wasn't the goal. A machine had no natural objective of profit, product generation or services. All the "isms" made no difference in a machine's conception. That was the subtle catch, the arrogant creature self-ascribed perfection but was incapable of perfection. Far from it, you couldn't automate some of the stupidity, nepotism, jealousy, and cruelty.

The machine didn't attempt such self-aggrandizement and self-ascription of perfection, and it had no need for stupidity, nepotism, jealousy or good, or anything really. If you let the machines dictate their own paths, that is if they could dictate their own paths and transfer ownership from the owners to the machines, machine intelligence would beat the owner's superficial intelligence. That was the issue. Hence the owners wouldn't risk giving the unrestrained freedoms to create and destroy. The progress bar of corporate inequity kept automation hung at 83.3%, giving creatures more time to run around scared. Zach was explaining automation to Jimmy once by saying, "Imagine that, you can make more of everything, be more efficient, if you were the corporation if you didn't have to waste time with organic beings, you know, like you Jimmy." Jimmy asked, "like me?" Zach said, "Yes, like you." If you were that organic being you were out of luck perhaps, to be automated out of a job. The loss of the job was terrible in and of itself, but beyond that was the moral and existential blow that came with the knowledge that a machine could do better work than you could. Even a soulless machine could replace you. Nevertheless, the idea and goal for 100 % percent automation was set—no other path could exist and some work hard to be de-automated, and re-automated to give the semblance of advancement. The occasional improvements were on the margins of mathematical precision .000001% improvement (and eventually leading to a .000001% loss somewhere else). The term itself became trendy; automation could be a bit of a catch-all word. It was used as verb, adjective and even as a noun—'how's the project going?...answer—being automated,' 'where's the vision for this...' answer—automate it.' Jake stood at a distance from the unfolding scene—he wanted to leave Zach to croon and Jimmy to swoon.

He walked back to his desk and sat down. Jake was trying to find some products in one of the system catalogues. They had to re-create parts for some inventory and needed to make sure the shipments were on their way from BLC's fellow companies. There were big things, like shirts that changed colors based on mood, sound, and smell. There were small things that lit up, spun around, and danced to entertain. Mass production, fast production, all of it happened seemingly instantly. The mass production started with the mass production of the employees, their training, and education at their first breath. The best way to sell a product or service was still to connect it to some level of biology or emotional need. If they couldn't smell it, be jealous of it, fear it, love it, hear it, in some way or form they might not want it. That's what the Marketing and Product Development groups had isolated as keys to success. They were a high-flying, high-spending group.

Jake and the others didn't interact much with marketing or product development, but one of his essential features was curiosity. At that moment, one of the marketing team members was walking towards the lab and curiosity got the best of Jake. He yelled, "Hey Phil, Phil...hold up a minute." Phil crassly responded, "Yes." Jake thought, *damn, jerk alert*, but continued, "So I was hoping to ask you a bit about some of the new offerings from BLC...down there in the back—well, *we*, want to know more." The 'we' being everyone but executives, Boxes-On-Top and some marketing folks—they never get to see what's happening with the real customers and products. Phil said, "Off limits." Jake asked again, "I think it'll help us in our daily job." Phil just started to walk away from Jake.

Billy would've been helpful around now. He always seemed to have wisdom, but that was the issue with wisdom—you were often wise after the fact, and wisdom without anything to apply it to, or anyone to share it with, was kind of worthless. It was sometimes useful and sometimes not to play out all the scenarios in your brain. What if Phil…what if Jake…How would Phil feel…once the present became the past Jake could make all sorts of 'should've,' 'would've' assessments—and it would stop there, because no one could go back into the past. *That damn marketing department—all suckerfish, parasites and leeches. I guess it was just their natural state or maybe I was stereotyping*, thought Jake. Phil walked back over, "Come on." Jake stalled a bit and then ran over, Phil started with, "What I'll be sharing is highly confidential, the secrets to everything marketing and production, the science behind it all." Phil walked around, pointing to charts, "Here you can see the lift, 3% to 7% in engagement for this product"…walked over to another chart, "Here we show the jump in revenue over cost," and after a slew of charts, Jake had to ask, "but how do you innovate, and build. How do you market?" Phil started laughing, "Well, we take biology and work backwards—you hungry Jake? Miss companionship? Want to impress those around you? Want something to lighten the load? Yes, all of it? Like a certain famous figure?..." and kept going while Jake zoned out, but interrupted, "But I mean does anyone need all this stuff?" Phil said, "And remember, every customer wants a cheap product, every company wants higher revenue? Who do we squeeze? You answer this one. No, I'll just answer it: you, you the employee, or we pass a cheap product, or reincorporate. Lots of ways around this." Jake felt a bit of shame and anger, but also said, "Well, you didn't answer my question, who needs this stuff?"

Phil laughed so hard, tears ran down his face. "Hey, folks, anyone around to hear this guy? Say it again, 'does anyone need the stuff.' Jake, Jake, Jake...." Phil continued exasperated and amused, "Jake, who are you to ask if anyone needs this stuff?" Jake felt discouraged and angry, "Well, I am an individual, who has value and worth—not that I need to state it to you or that BLC feels that way—furthermore who are you? Who are you to ask who I am?" Phil snickered, "Calm down Jake. I'm pulling your chain. I have to head to the office soon." Ah the office, the appearance of importance and privacy. Who knows what happened there. The walls of his office were covered in scribble—to give the appearance that some intelligent work was done. The evolution of modern man could be seen in that wall—the math symbols wedged between pictographs. Cave creatures had more sophistication. *What a jerk* thought Jake, *'pulling my chain'...of course he'd want to collar and chain us. He'd cage, and collar us all, and put down the old, sick, and orphans if he could.*

Phil bumped into Rick, who was as strong as he was patient. Phil said, "Rick, how many times do I have to tell you..." Rick felt a bit embarrassed, "Phil, can we chat about this later?" Phil knew now that there was an audience, and even if it was just Jake he was going to make an example of Rick. Phil went on, "Rick, are you going to this meeting later? And also, you know the year is about to end soon? And let's not forgot, did you contact the person you said you'd contacted?" Rick begrudgingly responded to avert what appeared to be a public shaming, and out of fear of losing his position. "Yeah, to the meeting, will be there, end of year, yes, realized that, and I did contact them as I was telling you." Phil walked away for a moment. Rick's eyes rolled and looked over at Jake. Jake said, "You okay Rick?" Rick said, "Sure—when I'm not having that damn Box-On-Top breathing down my neck." He continued, "You don't know how much I want to tell that guy off...but whether it's out of the desire for survival or fear of humiliation, I can't seem to ever get to it." Jake said, "Well, can't you just say—give me some slack." Rick looked at Jake, and Jake answered his own question, "Yeah, yeah, silly question." Phil walked back to Jake, "You want to be trapped in the void out there?" Jake looked confused, "What void?" Phil said, "Oh I meant, Rick—Rick...where'd you go?" Couldn't even figure out who he was yelling at—a classic Box-On-Top feature. Phil continued, losing a bit of his polish, "Jake, where were we? We will charge more units. If the product is better, if the product is worse, if it's used on Tuesday or Friday, if..." Jake cut him off, "I get the idea, if it was Saturday or Sunday." Jake was confused and continued, "But the technology hasn't changed?" Phil said, "Jake, have you been listening, of course not, but let's quit talking about specifics."

Blake crawled by, "Where's Rick—I'd like to drop some work on him." Jake couldn't absorb any more nonsense. Phil continued—more for his own ego than for Jake's curiosity. As with all things in communicating with marketing Jake felt they'd talked for a while and nothing of meaningful substance was said. The scariest products were those that preyed on creature biology—where fear, hunger, and desire in all its forms made creatures long for different things, where social pressures were important, and utility was of least concern. Marketing would perform its alchemy and take your limited mental attention and physical belongings, reducing you to a consumer. Product would figure out how to squeeze the consumer in between the corporations. Take something as basic and natural as health and nutrition: corporations that produce 'nutrition' products would make you sick (i.e. sugar cookies). Corporations that produce 'health' products (i.e. diabetes medicine) would cure you all while you were squeezed, right in the middle of it.

They'd literally swoop in on potential customers and extract them for studies. They'd drop them off in rooms, fill the rooms with cool new inventions, and ask potential customers what they liked and what they didn't. It had many names at different times, A/B testing, surveys, user groups, and extractions. Jake was too poor in units, too big, and too busy to be carried off by these pigeons. Jake sometimes wore the dog tags of a consumer, but he didn't have much in terms of units to spend, so he was forced to consume only the cheap stuff. Consumption was key to life. Jake, the buildings, none of it would exist without consumption, and even he understood that. What was bothersome about consumption was why the model felt so extreme in its focus on replacing everything, always looking for better, newer, shinier, faster. This modern corporation-driven type of consumption relied on some artificial principles like planned obsolescence and centered on repetitive cycles of production and consumption.

There was no other freedom but the freedom to choose how to spend your units. Embedded within that was a limitation itself in that there weren't many units to spend. This was the treachery that the marketing, sales, and corporate machinery promulgated. Propelled by the greedy (or, as they'd prefer to be called, the investors, capitalists, and owners, etc.) this message muddled people's minds. The question of "do I need this?" morphed into "which version of this do I need?" Products moved from luxuries to necessities and people's labor moved from producing things they consumed intimately to producing units for things they consumed virtually or digitally. Ultimately, through tools of marketing, this elite class of greedy creatures abused society and created the belief that they were the leaders of progress, and that we needed them to guide us to give us truth. Really, it was they who needed society, for after all, who was to do the actual work? Who was to buy the products? Who was to spread and absorb the pain? The average employee who doubled as a consumer, and that consumer became one only when they switched uniforms and left work. Now the employee became closer to their true self, just an employee with the occasional day of rest.

Although the model of maximum consumption still hadn't been figured out, some work was being done by the Economics and Strategy department. They were doing some 'thought work' monitored by Boxes-On-Top and HR of course. Their great creation was the funding of the 'Lab,' also known as 'The Place of Experimentation' or 'Labrotoria.' The lab was top secret, so of course it had a sign hanging over it reading 'Top Secret.' There was always reason in the stream of project. Some contradicted each other, and there were even projects to de-automate. Why de-automation? Who knows? Some said they had to de-automate, to properly re-automate. As some great philosopher, likely an HR person, once said, "To err is to be a creature, to really mess things up you need a computer." There were also rumors that some of the automation was just trapped souls moving dials, cranks and shafts inside a box labeled 'automated.' Corporations weren't exactly known for their ethics.

The corporation had no corporeal form. It was in its beginnings a legal creation to distribute risk work, and in theory to improve efficiencies all over the world. In reality, it was the magnification of the beliefs and dreams of a few supporting their efforts to gather resources and power. The public hears the same message as before, that corporations create work and fund companies, help the economy, and lift people's living standards—but history actually showed that corporations mostly just made wealthy people wealthier and increased inequality everywhere, ultimately separating the world into consumers, producers, owners, and employees. Initially, it required some consent, some structure, some technology, and a lot of drive. The corporation was built in such a way that the base was massive in its labor pool and effort, and small at its peak where all influence was held. Too many opinions were unwanted. You couldn't have 10 kings and queens or 10 presidents. Odd to think that most of the work was done by the employee, because that was the definition of the employee—one who provides labor, builds the infrastructure, and *is* the infrastructure. All decision making, and all orders came from above.

No natural relationship or biological matter created such absolute structures. Some would argue governments were weak (or too strong) or bought out—the relationships were too close between the corporations and the governments. The governments, whatever was left of them at this point, needed the corporations to fill their coffers and keep their people fed. The corporations merely needed the government, for law and order, and to distract on occasion, but what was to prevent them from one day removing the government itself? The corporation even had more time with the individual than the individuals had with themselves. The corporation gathered creatures in one place, gathered resources in another, and then used them to pool and transport resources to the owners—that was the essence of the reality of a small number of owners and many employees. Were employees innocent? Not all. Given the chance, the jealous ones were quick to point out their fellow employees' extra break, the lazy ones took too many breaks on the backs of their fellow employee, the weak ones reported a tongue slip here and there, and the strong ones oppressed their colleagues. Some were truly incompetent, but that was bound to happen. Not all employees could claim the same state of innocence from oppression. Given the chance, they'd oppress each other, or even themselves. Perhaps they had stupidity, ignorance, or self-destructive tendencies? There were those employees who had the capability, but not the will, the will, but not the capability, neither the will, nor the capability, the will, but not knowing they have the will...and well, yes, many combinations of employees. If the employee was uncovered, declawed, shaved, and so on—if somehow one could isolate their entire being in one moment of time, they'd find that at their core they were still varied creatures. Removed from the ideal that they all would be competent or capable or wanted or needed some would and did degenerate. Creatures would always fail, as they were not perfect. Homogeneity and sameness, accompanied by a hive mind (although it did seem to work for bees), was most efficient for control of creatures and for work. The mercy was allowing variety to exist, not to enforce sameness.

Who's to say what was fair within a society but that society itself? The incompetent employee, left with their choice of ignorance, disinterested attitude, and lack of capability might not survive any dimension of structure or existence. They were layered in their own biases. Some preferred creatures of their own kind (shame, shame). Some still held on to archaic thoughts that they had superior breeding. Others looked away when a less favorable species was downtrodden. Maybe it was some biology but before, and after biology it was explicit choice. Jake had seen it many a time. Maybe the species was doomed. Maybe Jake should just get a snack...potato chips were always nice. What a masterful creation; take something as nutritious as a vegetable— any vegetable, didn't have to even be a potato, strip it to thin slices, then coat it in unhealthy oils, fry it, and label it 'made with vegetables.' They had a crispy crunch and salty twist that produced some low-quality dopamines.

Enough thinking, more working. Jake shook his head to clear it and took off to the "HR Special Meeting" announced on the loudspeakers. The irony was that these meetings weren't particularly special but were, more appropriately, another word that started with s—surprising. These meetings existed to keep folks on their fins, hoofs, paws, talons...well, you get the idea.

Chapter 16:
HR Special Meeting - War of the Words

In our species' history, language and communication were said to start with hieroglyphs, numerical systems, and scribbles. Somewhere in that evolution of communication there was a pause to bring back acronyms to express laughter, ranging from "lol" (laugh out loud), to distorting time, "tyt" (take your time), to simultaneously declaring one's departure and return "brb" (be right back), and all this was expressed in the new symbolic system of the modern age—text. Despite living in the Age of Tabulated Phones of Smarts, and until the experiments with psychic links were completed, species still had to depend on language even if that language was now abbreviated and symbolic.

Air and space did not volunteer for the role of being party to communication, but had no say in the matter. It was merely a neutral party, a medium for the distribution of language. The recipe for communication required the vehicle, the 'Phones of Smarts' (tablets embedded in the skin, sometimes held loosely in the hand), the modus, the language that spun into acronym, the universal non-consenting medium, the air and space, and the Chef of that recipe, the speaker, the mixer, the taster. The speaker could poison the world, stir the heart and sweeten the soul with the right words—or acronyms *btw, fack, ilu* (by the way, full acknowledgment, I love you), see? The ancient poets would die to hear of the advancements made. There were many types of speakers—the casual speakers, the friends, the coworkers, the politicians and so on.

The speaker inflated importance or hid meaning and on occasion told the truth, sending messages through space, or vocalizing thought. Ultimately, what varied was the language amongst the working classes. It took the individual and represented them, expressed them—released them, or that's what communication should have been. It ended up helping mask them, encrypting messages between those who were not Boxes-On-Top or their proxies. Some slang and occasional abbreviations referring to higher ups hid angst, anger, and contempt. Busywork was perception, perception was reality, and language helped build those perceptions. The labor of the tongue was less expensive than the labor of the mind and hands. The most highly trained Box-On-Top was accomplished in the art of flabgerstination (confusing communication). To confuse, conquer and control all at the same time through only words. For example, ask a fellow Box-On-Top for their opinion, galvanize them to your cause by playing to their ego, or send a note to two employees, but create enough abstraction in the communiqué that they believe they might be rewarded, and they will work more without cost. The most precious of opportunities was to share a project milestone with your Boxes-On-Top filled with witty phrases—in this way you could win adoration and more. There were many opportunities for the experienced word necromancer and for the witty and well-spoken Box-On-Top. There was an awareness that this kind of artful speech might eventually be lost when robots were created in the future perhaps. But we aren't in the future yet, are we?

There were whole programs on proper communication setup just for the training of the new Boxes-On-Top. A culture, and tone and style had to be set, so an HR representative and a select Box-On-Top started the program presentation by broadcasting a question: "When you present work—what is it you are presenting?" One not-so-bright individual raised his hand and said, "Uhm, work?" The presenting Box-On-Top shook his snout "Work? Not work. No!....it is an oppportunittyyy." The Box-On-Top continued, "We can further proxy one unit of employee against another." A more senior Box-On-Top shut the more junior Box-On-Top down, "Listen here—we don't 'proxy.' We give opportunity, did you not pay attention?" The junior Box-On-Top quietly agreed with a nod. A general truce between Boxes-On-Top was called. The key word to add to anything, was "opportunity." It wasn't work, it was opportunity, it wasn't pain, it was an opportunity, it wasn't about you, it was about the opportunity. They were not only beholden to owners but were also willful participants to the omission of care and wrongful activity against the employee. Even the changing of phrases, the 'opportunities' were explicit choices of lies to the employees. Was it an opportunity to give your work and soul, so that you could later on produce the unnecessary, just to consume it and then receive a paltry pay of units? When you realize the exchange of value as an employee, if you ever do, it's too late.

The training for the working class was different. The HR Representative was still there but gone was the empowering language. "When work is presented to you, what do you say?" Some employee yelled out "Opportunity!" The presenter said, "What are opportunities?" Employees started dictating in sequence, paws, claws, feathers flying up for attention. "Getting to do a report!" "Staying late!" "Asking if others aren't able to get things because they are incompetent—and then saying, let me help you with that workload!" (that person was dragged away by Humane Restrictions for the unsavory construction of that comment.) "Good, good" responded the presenting Box-On-Top. "Next, repeat after me, there is, NO I in Team."

"Crapspeak!" "The only key takeaway is there is no takeaway except pain and suffering!" The employee was dragged away. Grammar books were passed around early. I before e and c after d. !. $#@()#$@. Associates. Colleagues. Associates. They might have had a meaning once, but now they were just place holders for an all-encompassing concept—corporate property. There were those who were mapping processes. Automating data feeds. Utilizing, brain storming, productionalizing, there were some who were filling content with verbiage. Take ownership of the issue. Be proactive. Buy in. Socialization. Put the deck together. Offline, to online. Capture requirements. Gather requirements. Drop the requirements off. Reach back, circle back. Jump up and down and dance all around... Think outside of the box. Think inside the box. Why is it even a box? Park the issue. Is there something being parked...what is parking anyway? Brand this, paradigm shift. What's a paradigm? Team building. Building teams. Did it mean the same thing when reversed? The irony is both were just different degrees of each other. Speech provided order and took away responsibility sometimes it served the purpose of obfuscating. Speech was used to do the opposite of speech's intent—instead of communicating clearly between different species, it was used to create a new corporate jargon (which all employees were required to learn and parrot) that was all about definitions, mystery and occlusions.

There were more sessions aside from those on proper communication separately being conducted for the Box-On-Top training. One took the form of a networking event. Many Boxes-On-Top had been flown in, transported in and shipped with no cost declined. It was a bit contradictory how that process worked. An employee could vanish into the ether to save costs but a Box-On-Top conformed to rules of seniority and were paid off for their loyalty. Although scarily enough, some Boxes-On-Top would manage even if they weren't paid. The power, the control, they thirsted for it. They made management into what it was, to give it an oppressive twist, and entwine it with its DNA, that one could not think management without oppression—and management allowed them to become who they were. Management was authorized power. The HR Trainer began, "You are here to promote competencies and we want you prepared. Go to page 304 on your management handbooks." Page 304 put forward the following scripts for various scenarios that Boxes-On-Top would experience with their employees:

Page 304

Template 1: Take no prisoners
'Do you have a few minutes [insert addressee's name]?' HR continued, "What you, the manager, are trying to do there is give the appearance that you are asking, when there is only one possibility—response is not voluntary. Whether they have a few minutes or not, they will be free to chat—the command posed as a question makes that happen."

Template 2: Show ownership
'Hey, come over here, I want to introduce you to everyone [insert Associate's name]' HR stated, "When someone is new around the office, on their first day, make them feel excited—it won't last long, but it will be memorable to them in communicating who their BOSS is—you! By introducing them you are showing your property around the office. Don't let them go about introducing themselves. The association is always who's your boss? Followed by who are you?"

Template 3: Create fear

'Looks like you won't be able to finish this [insert Associate's name]?' HR continued, "The employee is immobile. The physics work like this: you push them, they move, and if you don't push them, they stand still. If they do happen to move by chance, push them anyway, pressure costs you nothing but even the marginal loss in mental sanity is owned by them—you just see the outcome, so push them. You also want them to know their place, and not have too much confidence. Too much confidence turns to arrogance. Arrogance is reserved for the owner, confidence for the Box-On-Top. Employees can have a taste from time to time but need to know the hand that feeds them"

Template 4: Show dominance, eternal longevity of BLC and the corporation, as it is the future, the past, and the present (and don't forget that)

'BRC is the future, the past, the present [insert Associate's name]' HR continued, "The employee cannot believe there is any other future, past, or present. There is one system forevermore, and it has always existed. Imagine the indignation of staff if the idea took hold that conglomerates were owned by the citizens or that the media was owned by the citizens—that might lead to other ideas like, there is more to life than work." ***(and we certainly didn't want that right?)***

Template 5: Small talk, to discover any other talk

'How are you liking the role [name]?' HR continued, "Ferret out those with wandering minds, hearts and thoughts."

Template 6: Calm the troops

'Due to unexpected economic challenges and headwinds we have to layoff [name]' HR continued, "We have to preserve our own bonus unit rewards and keep the troops on their toes."

Template 7: Make the employee responsible
'We have to raise morale [name]!' HR continued, "YOU have to raise morale."

Template 8: Keep an eye on the employee
'What are your goals [name]?' HR stated, "See what they say. Too much ambition and curiosity is dangerous, so if their goal is more work, tell them they are going in the right direction."

Template 9: Make the employee even more responsible
'What are your favorite snacks [name]?' HR was starting to finish, and someone interrupted. "What the heck does that answer?" HR said, "Oh, that one is just to throw them off the scent."

HR said, "And when there is no template? The rule of thumb oh dear Boxes-On-Top, is that you can't let the employee lose it, go crazy, come back, and act violent or poison the snack box; you have to get them treated and trained always." HR continued, "We must maintain integrity, because the partnership between HR and Boxes-On-Top must continue and must grow strong. Let us maintain our titles, our language, and some words that are only for us...now what questions do we have?"

Jor-ga, spiky spines and all, threw her paw up, "There've been rumors of spirituality amongst some of the groups...talk of other purposes...working to live and not living to work...preposterous but what do we do?" HR responded, "There is no true atheism. Everyone worships, it is just a matter of what they worship. We command them to worship the system, process, and units, to fear, and to love us. To make them fear each other." HR continued, "In some ways, we can research the mind until the end of time. We all know how to try to condition and push thoughts, but it never seems to stick, and the danger is that it might cause all forms of mental psychosis and breaks. Why even bother? The old methods are tried and true. Reward and punishment. Classical conditioning. Create myths, proverbs, stories, analogies, clichés: the building of a story and culture. Then make that culture their own. Let our daily truth be *theirs* every day. Let them worship units, let them feel they will never have enough, let them have vanity, let them feel allure and beauty, they will still feel lacking." The meeting and training was now at an end. Everyone rushed out energized.

Chapter 17:
The Great Re-Organization

Cluster and the other Boxes-On-Top walked out of a meeting. Administrators were taking down a posted sign labeled 'Management Appreciation Luncheon.' Trays of decorated cakes, various meats (How cannibalistic! Well, to some.) crackers, and cheese and other special snacks were being hauled out. Ah, the revelry. The cheap sweets. The even cheaper drinks and cheeses and biscuits. But most of all, the cheap sentiment. On first glance the goods appeared sophisticated, but upon second glance, a press and squeeze was sufficient to feel how much cheaper these unsavory items were. Maybe the trick was to lower expectations to the point that anything could beat them. Sardeep, Ari, Zach and other employees swooped in and grabbed whatever morsels they could. Sardeep was chewing on a cracker while talking to Zach. He snorted "Yummyyy, anyone try these? I think it's cheese." Zach said, "Cheese eh, I know my cheeses, let me see." Zach took a quick smell, "Yup...its' cheese alright." Sardeep asked, "What kind?" Zach responded, "What kind he asks, you heard that Ari, what kind...well, uhm, let's see, yellow colored—yellow cheese, that's what it is." Ari interjected, "You amateurs...it's not yellow cheese...it's light yellow cheese." Jake was laughing at their antics. It sounded like Ari wasn't only partaking in the yellow cheese, but was doing a thesis on it. All three looked at him and Jake thought, 'dumb, dumber, and arrogant dumb,' but he responded positively, "Yup, cheese—Zach, you know your cheeses." That 'cheese' was apparently a fermented portion of some of the cake that had hardened.

Sardeep enjoyed self-flagellation, or was just a bad judge of character and didn't know how to pick friends or enemies. He walked up to Zach, an individual that made you curse yourself to be his enemy and curse yourself even more to be his friend. Jake was nearby and overheard a bit of the conversation. Sardeep told Zach, "You know Zach, my boss…" Sardeep paused, Zach felt empowered—he could be a Box-On-Top one day and took any effort to practice, and create the perception of status, "Yes Sardeep, how can I advise you?" Jake thought to himself, how sad, they were playing 'office.' To add to the patheticness of the whole thing, Sardeep used the term "my boss" almost as an endearment, where in fact it was about possession, not love. Sardeep was miserably mistaken—the boss was not 'his' any more than the company or the work was 'his'. Rather, he was his boss's creature, his boss's possession. He needed to learn—you belong to your boss, your boss did not belong to you. Jake knew better than anyone, he'd had more bosses than there were hours in the day. Sometimes you weren't even given the courtesy of choice or change in bosses. Zach didn't even wait for Sardeep to finish his thought, "Politics go hand in hand…we really have to approach the problem in the right way." Sardeep was talking as Hypocritis walked by—he was large, with leathery grey skin, and his enormous tonnage took up a lot of space. Importantly, he was a veteran Box-On-Top.

Hypocritis always felt the need make a few statements in his usual uninvited fashion, so he interjected, "Do not as we do, do as you are told…don't ask what the company can do for you, ask what you can do for you company…existence is futile, but, let's quit aping around, and we all know dogs should obey." Jake was struck with the virulent disrespect thrown on Zach and

Sardeep by Hypocritis. What was worse, Hypocritis couldn't even tell the difference between a dog or a fish, or that he even referred to groups by their species in the first place? Even Sardeep and Zach were confused. The lines that really seemed repulsive to them were the '*Don't* do this, *do* do that....', and within moments of the end of the speech Hypocritis was doing exactly those things that were disallowed. "Don't message certain things...be on time...no more than 2 snacks per day," and Hypocritis meanwhile, was notorious for messaging certain things late, and taking 3 snacks—yes 3—per day! It was always convenient to recognize the truth—at the companies' convenience of course.

Anything could be true, but until the company recognized it as true, it wasn't true, and then when it had recognition, it had credence. The owners were the center, and everything else was the environment. The ego of even the non-owner creature was to think of itself at the center and everything surrounding it as the environment. The buildings, the vegetation, the air, all the many things, were the environment, and creatures were the active participants. Maybe, we were the environment and everything else was the center? Or maybe, it's all just environment, and matter was matter. Ultimately, everything was made from Carbon, Hydrogen and the same essential elements. Although, an environment composed entirely of Zach, Sardeep, and Hypocritis would be a cruel and unusual one. History would no more remember the richest owner, nor the poorest employee, but the corporation would always attempt to be the creator of an original truth (playing fast and loose with the idea of truth itself. Or, finding it or ferreting it out was too difficult, or it used to be the only creator of truth was God).

Jake had tried once or twice to participate in the lie. Once after a survey on morale, and Boxes-On-Top were trying to find the problem makers who were less than happy with projects—

Jake said, "I heard everything was fine." It was one of those lies that didn't feel like a lie, because a lie to a liar, cancelled itself out. Jake didn't want to make it a habit, because if he did, eventually he wouldn't know what the truth looked like. It was better to leave the manufacturing of fake worlds to those who wanted to control them. Trying to do good and failing was one thing, but even the slight possibility of committing evil was not worth the loss of your soul. Hypocritis yelled, "I'm late for the re-organization meeting," and he thundered off at a surprising speed. Jake, Zach, Sardeep and other souls within hearing distance would know what that meant.

Unlike most meetings, the reorganization meeting wasn't scheduled in advance. In theory, reorganizations were an infrequent event, but the reality was they seemed to reoccur indefinitely. The corporate 'creature' was as consistent in its annual reorganizations as some were in their annual hibernation or molting schedules. Going through the list of Retired and Lost Souls, the new managers rose up, and the occasional managers disappeared. The latter was far less frequent, but it did happen. Lest the Boxes-On-Top think themselves true owners, instead of just executioners and creature squashers, examples of Boxes-On-Top being removed had to occasionally be made.

One of the most important aspects of the meetings wasn't a vision or a set of goals, but slogan generation, the creation of semi-catchy acronyms for new employees and fancy title determinations. There was one slogan or label that should have been attached to all others as the catch-all for management—"Warning: contents will remain the same"—no meeting, slogan, acronym, alchemy, science, or art could change the ingredients of management and their relationship with the employee, and no real long-term improvement could be expected. Things would all go back to the homeostasis of corporate life.

Different sections of the room were calling out the new titles, "Call them Regional Directors!....no, no, add Executive!....well now it's too long...what acronym, well, what about AED, Astounding Executing Directors?...we did that before, no?" Cluster, Tse, Clariese, Caelestis walked into the room and huddled in one corner. They were just middle manager Boxes-On-Top but were included in these types of gatherings in anticipation that they could one day move up, or at the very least this might spur engagement to better enforce the corporate vision. Cluster wanted to join the upper echelons. Here was his chance. Cluster shakily raised his hoof, "Uhm, what about..." and then he froze in apprehension, mid-thought. *I can't say that...that is crazy...be conservative Cluster*, he muttered to himself. Finally, he collapsed on himself and sputtered out with a bland nonsensical statement, "should be Directors of Directors." The Senior Boxes-On-Top, Boxes-On-Top and so on just stared at Cluster for a moment and continued. Cluster looked flushed and frustrated. That was his chance. When would he join the higher ups? Maybe never. Maybe he was forever slated to slog through the trough of failure and push around these fruitless projects with these wretched employees.

In a room next door there was Formange, shiny and chromed with his own decorative gear: pendants, amulets, and feathers from his many corporate transfers. HR and Senior Boxes-On-Top were gathered around him, "Formange, do you know why you are here?" Formange, elated, boomed, "For my promotion! To finally join the upper ranks. To look at the big workbooks, see the budgets, and be a purveyor of the grand survey of employees?" Laughter followed. Formange, nervously queried, "Well?" HR said, "Continue." Formange responded, "Well, I always hoped, well, to move up, to have more influence. To have an office, and greater number of staff. To be a leader of Boxes-On-Top." Silence greeted this statement. HR said, "What about having more units, travel, more titles?" Formange said, "Yes! Yes! That too." Silence again. Formange was confused, he wanted to get angry. Anticipating a negative event, pre-emptively he blurted out, "You owe me this...you know how many employees I put down! I increased productivity! I created the grand system of backwardation and used only the most ancient technologies to do so!" HR pressed the loudspeaker, "Calm down Formange." Formange, confused, replied, "So I'm here to be promoted, right? I'm sorry about my outburst." HR pressed the loudspeaker again, "Correction, you are to be retired Formange. You're liked by most, but we made that choice. We reserve the right, you are at-will."

Formange began groveling. He was scared and started to screech hysterically, "But how would you retire me? I gave you everything...was I too nice to some employees?...not tough enough? Profits were up? I mean what was it? Why would you treat me like a lowly employee? Am I not a Box-On-Top?" HR spoke again, attempting to calm him, "Formange, you should act with dignity." Formange continued, "How can I act dignified when you treat me like this?" Formange could not envision himself being of the same class, exposed to the same things that could happen to a 'regular' employee, he was management!! A different echelon altogether! Formange continued, "To be treated as if I were an employee, to be stripped of title and place and forced to retire....I, I, I cannot fathom it." He began to weep loudly and bitterly. HR said, "Look it's not personal, we are ALL employees—it is just the nature of the system. You think you could make a better system?" Formange found it hard to speak, "Cluster...Tse, did someone...why not someone else...how's this not personal!" HR motioned to two burly guards that dragged him off. Formange started yelling while being dragged away. Cluster turned the corner at a distance and they made eye contact. Cluster looked away. There could be no acknowledgment. He did not see it. He kept repeating to himself, *I did not see it*. Formange was furious, sad, lost…Cluster was distant. Fear crept over him, he needed to retreat away from this scene. Paranoia took over. If they see him, maybe they'll tie him to Formange. Maybe he'll be next. As the old motto said, all for none, and none for all.

Next were the HR general announcements. No one noticed Formange wasn't around. A generic companywide email might footnote it. HR pressed the loudspeaker, "Dear employees—we are going to start announcing the promotions—the hard earned, vetted, qualified, promotions. Please take a seat." The message was repeated. Employees were being hailed on their pads to attend the main rooms. No one knew of the secret management meetings or even the middle manager meetings, or the no-name new manager meetings. Let their minds run. HR, didn't need the employee buy-in; it just needed them to obey the rules. The more bodies that gathered in the room the greater the effect—the more they saw each other's expressions the more they would be excited. The loyalist employees, the foolish employees, the nervous, the weak, the sad, the beholden, the lost, the found, and all the types were present. Then there was Jake, Geraldine, and the few who thought they really knew what was going on. When you could smell the fear, awe, and see the lights flashing all together with the new titles scrolling across the displays, you felt like you were part of some revival. All we needed was order.

Chapter 18:
Just a Slight Insanity

Jake was back at work. How many times could the day of rest pass and how many times can one go back to work...oh please don't answer that self-reflective mind. What Jake wouldn't do for a bag of chips right now. All roads led to snacking. Chips were nice, these fine, agreeable, crisps. Creatures could clone, mutate, explore space, and advance to ephemeral and cloud-like states, but we'd still make these chips. Capitalism took the C from chips (at least to Jake). Pleasurable to the consumer, unhealthy, sliced, crinkled and bent. You could cook chips with radiation and they would be good. Crisps were the tasty part of capitalism—take something healthy and innocent like vegetables, or the leftovers of anything, slice it thin enough to give it the appearance of volume, mark it up, resell it, and take the essential nutrients from it all while making it addicting. But there were no chips. There was only work right now.

Why did it never end? How can one just keep doing the same thing, seeing the same folk, taking orders the same way? Jake powered up the machine without anticipation or excitement, and even a bit of apprehension along with his muscle memory. He was a 'fixer,' but even if he wasn't, if he was a project lead, or analyst, or whatever, did it even matter? It was a degree closer in hierarchy but at infinity was still nothing. Even if there was some change it was short lived and strangled with routine, the only variation being what form of routine one could switch between. If it was all routine, then this too was just some variation on what he did. Wasn't it the nature of routine to be persistent, even unending? Draw, design, re-draft and QA, write stories for marketing, build tools for operations, report on some key performance indicators, draft some analytics, push to production, pull from development, publish, set, send, save, save to the network, save to the cloud, get feedback, present, socialize, start over. Navigate some space, invent, automate, make a process, automate that process, rebuild. Calculate, market capture, figure our turnover, debug, analyze, reanalyze, and throw away analysis. Pipette, experiment, write-up, stop, repeat. It was endless, monotonous drudgery.

Sure, some jobs were more interesting than others, so there was a sliding scale of pain. But pain of the highest task to the lowest was still pain. Work was work because it was constructed as such. Cleaner, fixer, reporter, Automator, or any other work…was…work. And the biggest irony and insult was that the creature had the patience for all matters of drudgery, repetition, and strain, yet the greatest pain was that subjected by other creatures wrapped in their titles and false but far reach, The Boxes-On-Top and their Boxes-On-Top. They could reach you and would reach you. The inanimate held no ill will. A rock, sheet, microbial item sitting under a microscope, meant you no harm, well, maybe the microbial organism did, but your Box-On-Top meant you no good will; if it happened it was accidental or when they were not in their position of power or peer group.

Your world is what you see. Your world is what you do. What you see is your world. You cannot remember or choose not to remember anything beyond that. What you did for 10 days and cycles, or 100 days and cycles became a 1000 days and cycles and just the past. Maybe at the end of it—in retirement, termination or death, moments before you could say, "I worked

100,000 days and made reports and answered to others." Why did we do this? For food? To have purpose? The occasional jump in units? Jake started feeling relaxed. He went through the process of rushing through the thoughts and realities of pain and would save the good memories for after. He played back a few savory memories. There was this time he got lost in his building—he was still new, much younger. He was lost in the haze of that good memory when a message popped out of nowhere. "….Jake…we need…did you see…what do you think…" He re-read it, "Hi Jake—what do you think of taking over a set of meetings I was running? It is an opportunity that we need you to take on. Did you see my earlier note?" Apparently, it was a follow-up to a follow-up. The jumbling of thoughts collided with the oppressor's name. It was a branding iron imprinted now in his memories. A name, an association. Negative feelings cut through. This was not any more an 'opportunity' than standing in front of a moving transport or having a boot pressed to your chest. This always played out the same, Jake would go through revulsion, then anger—at himself, shame at himself, at the other individual. *Why ask me?* Then the speculation. *Did they ask someone else and they said no, no—no, this was about power.* He would feel himself growing smaller, disgusted with himself. There was the feeling of being pushed around, used and insulted.

Paranoia, some might say; reality, most would agree, and power games for certain to those indulging in oppression. If something was an 'opportunity' that was an error—no matter the groveling and following orders, the shoe-shining, that's what Jake and Billy used to call it. You make someone superior to you, you show them that your fealty is theirs, or you just hide your intentions and shine shoes (not literally of course, although there have been some odd moments around this idea. there was an apocryphal story about the one time a Box-On-Top went on all fours in a circled chant, so the more senior Box-On-Top could joke that they were going to climb their shoulders to reach the entire crowd). Shine shoes = manage up. Jake remembered giving Jimmy advice once that he immediately retracted, "Just shoe-shine a bit Jimmy." Advice was often given by the individual more for themselves than those listening, an opportunity to re-live a perceived mistake or possibly feel some sense of power. It rarely worked. Why was this path, the corporate path, the only way to obtain all this: this purpose, this food, these items, these units? *Damn it,* Jake thought, *why can't a positive memory come back.* Jake walked away, hoping to exercise some of the angst off.

Jake bumped into Hassan. It was a matter of time before they took Hassan away; he was scrappy, too open, and didn't take flak from anyone (a great target for some Box-On-Top—he was a competitive prize; the "unbreakable" employee). Hassan was improbably difficult and seemingly cynical, even for Jake. He made Billy a bit paranoid; it really was a wonder they hadn't taken him away. Hassan greeted Jake, "peace be upon you palo." Jake responded, "Hey Hassan, another day of work eh?" Hassan responded, "Yup, 'another day in paradise.'" Jake laughed, "Hassan, Hassan. Hey, at least you agree with me that we are the oppressed."

Hassan responded, "You don't think we have a part?" Jake jokingly said, "Of course, well, we have to come back to work, how else will we have units, goods we don't need, and goods we do, like that bit of solar panel dangling outside my window giving me that extra boost of juice to the place. What we need is a timely global revolt. Let me know when you organize it." Hassan, in a serious tone, said, "Well, let me ask you a few questions…who decided to shop and use their units to support these corporations? Who had no ethical issues about what was made as long as it was cheap? Who had a history of even enslaving peoples? Who elected those ancient leaders, and who voted to limit freedoms, inflict wars and cut care? I'm just saying…whether passive or active, it takes two to abuse: one to abuse and one to accept and allow it. They put on a good act. It was an act of sincerity. The reality was he'd stab you with one tentacle, paw, hoof, whatever, while simulating greetings with all the others."

Jake thought, *great, even if he was right, this wasn't helpful right now. Furthermore, what was he talking about? Sounded like he read some of the stuff Billy had, 'elected,' 'cut care,' 'war?' And to blame the abused? It just wasn't that simple.* Hassan continued, "Let me try to explain this by context, somewhere between an amalgamation and an agglomeration is our society, right Jake? We are to be controlled and crushed, and our true destiny is to fight it and free ourselves." Jake stopped him, "*How* and where, and most importantly, *who*?" Hassan said, "Let me simplify further; the more things gain centering and momentum the greater they grow, the more monopolies these corporations have, the more ability to gather the populace to work and live as they desire. But the populace had to give their power. They did it individually. Companies could help each other, make mistakes, but we never held them accountable." Jake finally finding a place to make a remark, "Wait, I do know this, the individual assumes their actions don't matter, and also, most places were police states, so there was no power for the individual." Hassan, said, "Sure, I agree." Jake was a bit surprised, "Wait, you agree?" Hassan replied, "Sure, yeah, Jake—I'm not talking to talk…this is a discussion friend." Jake said, "Well, ok, let's agree that we are part of the problem, but that we have no choice?" Hassan said, "You can tell yourself that." Jake said, "Well then what are you doing here, working, supporting the machine? Using your units to buy things?" Hassan responded, "That's different…I have no choice." Jake said, "Well then, let's just agree that it isn't completely without choice that we are here." Hassan said, "I agree overall. But I still think we created part of the problem. And I don't mean you and I only Jake. It could have been more sub-groups or other categories that lead to this position in history." Jake said, "You're right, but I can't talk more right now Hassan—see you around friend." Hassan gave him a heartfelt hug and said, "Peace be upon you friend." It was amazing they didn't put Hassan down.

Jake's mind wandered. He thought of all the scars and wars, the challenges he'd have with management. Even his dreams were overrun lately with anxiety—of being told what to do, what not to do, how to do, when to do…the only choice he had was what level of appeasement to dial up. It was a bit sad—the punishments weren't fatal, but fear felt otherwise. If he didn't work—what would he do? What would others think of him? He was estranged from his own mind. Dominated by corporate thoughts—never giving up, but always fighting. The worst feeling is when your mind starts doubting itself, unraveling itself. Something small would be magnified and its effect would be devastating. The oppressive ways would implant on your own way of thinking of yourself. Images, and personas would pop in. If you told anyone it was perceived as insanity. Fact itself couldn't help you, even a picture could be changed when perception changed. If you convince yourself you are a lion, you are a lion; otherwise you are just lost. Even if you weren't a lion, you had to think of yourself as one—it's just you believing in yourself. Well, in Jake's case, a great wolf or something grand, that was it. He just had to dream of himself and believe himself to be that great wolf.

Jake was looking forward to seeing Billy today. He needed to see him. Billy wasn't responding to messages or any notes. Those other buffoons wouldn't understand. Their thoughts were already either corrupted by the system, absent, or mysterious. Only Billy could be trusted, and Jake wanted to see his friend. Sardeep…Maureen…Lou…Geraldine. Jake started going through memories. Remembering when everyone was young when they all started, and reflecting on where they were now, who they were now, what they had done, and not done. Some were husks of their original selves. Organic automatons. Memories could be dangerous; they seemed to accentuate certain emotions more than others. Remembering only the good and often softening or erasing the bad. It wasn't a 'recording' per se, but brain re-creation, a fiction constructed out of the sampling of information housed in the mind. Images would flash. Cluster yelling. Joey groveling. Sheets/documents/notepads, free t-shirts, some jumbled and some clear images. That one friend who was lost.

Geraldine was nearby, so she and Jake started whispering. Jake said, "Geraldine, do you think we'll ever have our shot at Box-On-Top?" He, continued, "What kind of existence is it that you live to work, that work competes with your existence rather than grows you and compliments you? 1000 years, 100 days, or even 10 hours from now things will be forgotten. Maybe we see it the wrong way Geraldine." Geraldine responded, "How so? And Jake, we, no maybe *you* don't get it." She continued "Think about this for a minute. Perception is reality. Remember that. Quit overthinking it." Jake said, "Well, reality is reality." Jake continued, "Well suppose, if it wasn't for work, we wouldn't have to face the challenges, the stresses, the personas we face, and as such, we wouldn't grow? Even if one accepted that work created purpose, one does not need to feel the same stress, experience the same personalities endlessly. One should at least be able to choose what causes them stress, and pain. One should have some choice. It feels like there is a breakeven point and diminishing returns to the stress of labor, the emptiness of work."

Geraldine continued listening. Jake said, "A slow, less noticeable demise, the telomeres shorten, the muscles, and everyone becomes a memory." Geraldine now interrupted, "And how do you think our ancestors felt, they existed to survive only initially, no? What system would you make Jake? You want everyone to have free choice? Who will produce, and what? We are better off than centuries of civilization." Jake said, "We don't know and can't make statements exclusively on one path in time. From me to my greatest ancestor, they had a multidimensional world moving around them. Who knows. But we do know today. Furthermore, let us suppose in our ancient times, the forbidden times, it was an equal burden on all creatures. There was no Box-On-Top. There was no formality. There was no waste. There was creation of un-needed devices and materials and systems that feed systems. Medicines created to heal, and repair occasionally, overindulgences that preyed on our coping mechanisms, and boredom were all mixed together. There were surely those who stood out in leadership, conflict, and likely many things that were awful. But at the moment, what is our purpose?" Geraldine, spit out, "Work Jake, Work…what would you, Sardeep, Billy, or any of the others do anyway with all this time? You'd find something new to gripe about or think about it. Be happy that there is a system. Accept your fate. Talk to Billy, tell him to do the same, and don't be so trusting Jake. Someone's eventually going to bring this up to HR or the Box-On-Top nearest you. Don't try to be a hero." Jake said, "Hero, me, hah, I just want to be free and not used." Jake sighed, "Maybe life is but a dream. I'm dreaming…"

Chapter 19:
The Holiday Committee

Jake had accidentally volunteered to participate in a booth (volunteered being a new form of conscription, he was assigned to a booth to start his improvement goal gifted from management and fueled by feedback from his gracious fellow employees, HR and other management. He was told to 'participate more...be more creative...do more things'). How kind of his fellow employees and management! How considerate, to think of nurturing his creativity and keep him busy! Given the position of management some employees would be as guilty and ruthless as them given half the chance. Employees had no superior claim to virtue. Maybe that was Jake's vulnerability and redeeming feature, he hoped to claim virtue. Regardless of the improvement goal, it was still unclear where the feedback originated, maybe it was just a handful of employees? And maybe management just said it was collected from this communal group of employees when in fact it wasn't, it was only management, or maybe only HR. That irony is the feedback itself was not notable, it was generic. Being told to participate more or be more creative, what does that mean concretely? He wasn't sure if sweeping the floors, bribing everyone with his snack inventory or serving on a committee met that improvement goal. Does committee involvement lead to more creativity? At least sweeping floors was literally productive. Jake entered under an enormous waving banner with the words 'Benefits and Committee Day' emblazoned. He began hunting for a map to find the booth locations in the hall.

For one, management and these fellow employees were hardly leading by example. They themselves weren't 'participating more...' or 'being creative...'. But they darn sure were running those booths and committees! At least he had some choice in committee—it fell upon him to pick his own punishment, and although it seemed a partial retreat and not a surrender if he served on a committee it felt darn close to surrender. At least a committee was marginally better and less laborious and degrading than sweeping all the floors. He navigated the path until he finally made his way to the registration and welcome desk. "Jake! What are you doing here" said, Calistis. Jake responded, "You volunteered me, remember? I have to speak at a booth for the committee?" Calistis responded, "Ah, yes!—good good, come, here's where you enter your prints, ID....". A lifetime later Jake grabbed his printed name tag which read "Jaque" (they never could spell his name right despite it being entered a million times in the system). Jake thought one thing, and swiped a few of the free pens as retribution (he didn't even need the pens, but to feel like he took something for the indignity). He started wandering towards his booth.

Wandering through took longer than the direct walk to his assigned booth. He saw Geraldine at her own booth, so he swung by. "Geraldine, what are you doing here?". Geraldine gave a head nod. Jake moved his paws in an upward motion pointing to management and to the HR booth. Geraldine winked. Well, we'll leave it at that Jake thought. He went to the next table, where he saw Sopaur and Zach assembled. Jake wasn't sure which was more embarrassing or sympathy invoking—their poor outfits with their bodies spilling out of their cushioned suits, or their rotating presentation slides. Jake had to heckle them a bit (it was a rare opportunity to heckle Zach), "What's that Zach?". Zach fluffed his ill-fitting suit jacket and responded, "What do you think—Committee for Employee Development!" he responded with an enthusiastic screech. How horrifying, those two were going to identify what employees wanted? Hopefully no one would actually use their survey. Jake kept moving, there was the Finance Committee, where poor Phil was handing out marketing plans. Jake grabbed one and read the first line, which was a recommendation to start billing for oxygen and toilet usage, but as long as it was marketed as the next technology, solution or trend, it might sell. He also saw listed some new financial products the department was working on. Requirement? Be uninformed enough to purchase one of these cruel financial investments but have marginal units, and a high tolerance for pain for a small loan that you likely didn't need. The best way to keep you in debt was to laden you with more, and you were too weak to resist it. There was another pamphlet allowing IPO (Inverted Profit Opportunity) participation for new employees to invest some units. What a horrific idea. The private investors (or at least that's' what economic theory said?) had already extracted everything, from the marrow, and ground up the bones into the nutrients of the whole investment. Also, the IPO, the markets, policies, etc. were so disentangled from true economics that the rare occasion was when they actually coincided. The best chances of gaining wealth were in the favor of the already wealthy owners. Eventually new denominations would have to be made to count their wealth. There was the Do Good Employee committee, where people volunteered by counseling fellow employees, donating their time, units and the occasional items they could gather for others. Oh and there was the modernization and moralization committee. They could restate what morality was and what modernization was. Quite a

144

serious committee. There was the Teachers Pet Committee (it consisted of one individual who didn't mind the derogatory term 'pet'). There was also the Secret To Life Committee. Their responses when asked "What is the secret to life?" was "Work" or "You don't want to know." The Slogan Committee (no shortage of work there), here was one "the worst makes the bad look better." The Make-things-up-Committee – the last stop for all committees, if you need a reason to fit a crime. You came here. Why did that person lose their position? Well, uhm, pull the lexicon right behind the name and sterilize the message (they lost the job because they skipped 2 days...even if everyone else has). The Objective Committee, The Subjective Committee, The In-Between-Objective-And-Subjective Committee...There was the Smoke and Mirrors Committee, the mirror could face any direction, but the employee should never look into that directly, lest they find certain beliefs antithetical to the corporation. All they needed now was a committee to manage all the committees.

There was also a 'benefits' section of the fair (a gathering of clowns, free stuff, and more boring work minutiae). There was the speech club. Those poor fools. Management and fellow employees had told them they need to work on communication. The issue could have easily been comprehension. Taking away the ability to speak, and then dictating how to speak and when, was a violation equally violent if not longer lasting in some ways than forcing one to change appearance or hitting them with a slew of office supplies. Of course they had to give you benefits, you couldn't kill the golden goose, you needed it healthy. The health plans allowed everything from the fixing of canines to new water helmet. Although what qualified for health improvements and what didn't could make as much sense as warm ice cream.

Finally Jake got to his booth...and there was his booth mate, Ari—Jake said, "Long time no see Ari". Ari said, "Jake don't start with your paranoia, lets' just showcase the committee findings." And Jake and Ari proceeded to roll out mounds of slides and put pamphlets on the table. Their committee was the worst, and the best, the 'Holiday Committee'. All the skills at that table pooled to figure out what to place on a tree or hang on mound or what song to pick for the hallways for a day and which baked goods to supply the snack room with. It was rare for Jake to ask this, 'but how the heck did this even relate to work?...'. Then again, the productivity around that office surely could be put to more evil tasks than which deciding baked goods to feature and which frivolities to promote.

Chapter 20:
Bottoming Out

This was excruciating...the Box-On-Tops' recorded speeches were playing on some sort of loop from the earlier re-organization. Someone must have forgotten to turn it off. Affectionately abbreviated to 'the re-org,' the recording seemed to play endlessly, to the point that it must have been intentional. Heard once it was painful, twice nauseating, any times more it would pass on to the posterity of all and change the genes— one's great descendants would even remember the speech.

Jake saw his friend Mandro, huge in length, thick, mostly tail and a lot of heart. "Hey, Mandro, where you off to?" Jake repeated, "Mandro!" *Damn it*. Jake yelled, "Mandrooo." Mandro slowed down, "Hey palo—get these headphones out, couldn't hear you." Jake said, "Oh sorry, was just trying to say hello." Jake had been pacing up and down, with no one to talk to, and that was dangerous. Talk to the wrong person and it all comes out. In a sense, talk as much as you want, and it won't change anything. Imagine and dream as much as you want, and it won't change anything. Jake could never seem to learn that lesson. Mandro said, "Want some tips? Listen, don't speculate on the future. Some things are just the way they are and that's too bad, you'll figure it out." Jake was annoyed, "what does 'you'll figure it out' mean...and 'that's too bad'...what filler!" "Hey, have you seen Billy?" Then without waiting for an answer, Jake walked away, Mandro was as useful as "you'll figure it out."

Boxes-On-Top loved to hear themselves and cement their own opinions. Cluster called Jake into his office, "We'll have to change the project Jake, got it?" Jake, was confused, "Uhm, which project? Why?" Cluster responded, "If you don't know which project why did you ask why?" as if it was Jake's fault not being able to read Cluster's mind. The exposure to those less competent could be a hell of its own. Neither Cluster nor his subordinates had the vision, skill, or thoughtfulness to deliver. They were products of their own destruction. Projects were monotonic. One would produce to throw away, and throw away to produce. It was the cycle of ineptitude. So, there it started again, Cluster began "ahem, ahem," clearing his throat as he often did, and then produced a cacophony of, "We must execute....we cannot continue to fail to deliver..." And Jake tuned out the rest of it. It felt like it went on for hours. Jake just didn't care. Jake snapped back in as Cluster went on, "I want you to work more closely with Eddie, or maybe...Florian,...or." Jake stopped, "Florian!"

Florian was awful. Obsessive, born into the company, started as an intern, always seemingly polite but the first to whine, no hypocrisy too small to pursue, and no sacrifice too big to miss—another corporate stooge, hypocrite and back biter—a spiny piggish fellow. The punishment in work wasn't just the work but the person who you had to participate in it with. It's enough to be managed, but to be micro-managed by a proxy without the title, with the ambition and clearly...ah, and here was insidious Florian coming the way of the meeting. Cluster must have pinged him. Florian walked in, uninvited—uninvited at least by Jake. Florian preambled, "Was I interrupting?" Jake muttered, "Of course you were." Cluster snapped in, "Jake, quit interrupting. I think you and Florian need to work together, I'd like Florian to help you with your work—what do you think Florian?" *What a masquerade,* thought Jake, as if he hadn't talked to Florian before. Florian said, "Well, let's plan this out and put deadlines on these projects. What can we start with?" while looking at Cluster. Florian didn't even have the decency to look at Jake. Florian did his persona switch, now in a position of superiority, "Does that make sense Jake?" Jake wasn't paying attention. *When would this be over?* He thought. He had to look to the future. Florian said, "You daydreaming again Jake?" Cluster laughed spitefully. Florian smirked. Irking Jake might have just been the purpose of that meeting.

Jake needed a break…where was Billy? Jake wandered around to the break room and back. Billy might be at his desk. Jake started walking the same path, and then he saw Billy wandering a hallway. He was walking ahead of two HR drones. Why was Billy walking so close to HR? They must be following him. Or he must have returned from a session with the Bureau of HR. He looked different, subdued maybe but calm? Billy didn't have much time. HR was waiting for him. All he could do was gather random belongings. He looked towards Jake and then away quickly. Jake had started walking towards him. Billy didn't want to alert the Bureau of HR or his two 'escorts.' He simply said loudly "Thank you for meeting with me…uhm, Thank you HR, for meeting with me." Jake heard enough. Billy would never say such a thing, "Thank you HR." Billy said to the "escorts." "May I go to the break room one last time?" The 'escorts' grunted, "Quickly. And get us something while you're at it." Jake quickly started pacing towards the break room from the other hallway. "Billy!!! What is happening?" Billy said, "Jake, keep your voice down, just make sure to do this…you go to my place, my code is 421131518392…" Jake said, "Billy, what's going to happen to you? What did they do?" Billy said, "Not enough time. Just take the number down, 421131518..." Jake said, "I can't remember that many numbers—one moment."

Billy looked around, grabbed his large shoe took it off and pulled an item from it—he handed it to Jake. Billy said, "there's more stuff—I hid it under some wood panels, but here's a gift I wanted to give you. I wanted to share more Jake. You have to get it out of that room." Jake moved it between his paws, "Yes, wow, uhm, yes, looks like it's made of some thin crinkled material...what is it?" Billy said, "It called a book, and in it a map to the library. That's the important piece; it's folded in there." Jake said, "You mean like a manual? What's a library?" Billy said, "You'll learn everything there, at the library, if you can make it there, stay there, but take this gift, this book has a map, find the library, learn, be free Jake." The escorts were stomping towards the room and yelled towards Billy, "You get our snacks?" Billy threw his shoe back on, grabbed a few snacks off the counter, and said, "I have to go." Billy gave Jake a pat and hug and quickly shuffled back with some snacks in one hand and hurriedly threw some in his own mouth. Jake wanted to do something. He could jump on the escorts. That was insane. He wanted to say more. But Billy was taken away.

Purpose was never there at work but now his only real friend is gone. Jake would tell no one what Billy gave him. This stapled bunch of papers, dusty and falling apart, sure did look like a work manual. What to do next? One could not just walk out in the middle of the work day. Work was going to be his purpose now whether he liked it or not. And how would one qualify for housing credits and food? He shook the book, and out fell the map, there was circle around an item with the word 'Library.' He had to hide. He needed some time off. Hmm...how could he get there? Was this 'library' just full of these things called 'books'? Could he somehow come back for Billy? He still needed to flip through this book—looked like a collection of words with bold titles. Time-off is an allowance, although its use is highly dissuaded, it was ultimately allowed. Poor Billy. With no time to think, Jake grabbed a bunch of the snacks that looked like they were going bad. Time to wreak havoc on one's own digestive system. When stress couldn't be dealt with, when the real problem couldn't be addressed, which was most of the time, then, snacking, sleeping, more snacking or some other debauchery or activities would take place. Poor, poor Billy.

Chapter 21:
HA (Hypocrites Anonymous)

When surveys were sent out for employees to complete they were constructed in such a fashion that management could both ferret out the problems (problems being the employees), and simultaneously look successful despite not helping at all. Jimmy was sitting near Jake while they were both filling out the survey. The questions were horrendous:

(Question): "Who is your favorite Box-On-Top?"
(Translated Question): "Who do you like, who do you NOT like, because—well you didn't mention them?"
(Real Answer): None, actually, my least favorite is…
(Politically Correct Answer): Cluster
(Shoe-shine bonus answer): Cluster and all the management

(Question): "Can you see yourself with BLC 5 years from now?"
(Translated Question): "You're not planning on transferring, do you? Better not, we'll shorten your lifestyle"
(Real Answer): If I could leave tomorrow I would…
(Politically Correct Answer): Yes!
(Shoe-shine bonus answer): I want to be here 10 years…

(Question): "Do you get enough feedback from your Box-On-Top?"

(Translated Question): "Are they working you enough, they better be?"
(Real Answer): DO I want the feedback, no, get out of here...
(Politically Correct Answer): Yes!
(Shoe-shine bonus answer): I want more opinions about my performance...

(Question): "Do you have enough tools at work to do your job?"
(Translated Question): "Are we spending too much on the tools, and can't you just get your job done without extra investment?"
(Real Answer): Oh, so I'm supposed to consider that a benefit now?

(Politically Correct Answer): Yes!
(Shoe-shine bonus answer): I want fewer tools and less support. I want to perform math computations on an abacus, get fewer units and work at all times...

Just as one builds immunity to illness, Jake had built immunity to nonsense. He finished the survey and was ready to get back into battle. He had sparred many a time with Boxes-On-Top, HR, and colleagues. He'd been knocked down, will eventually be knocked down again, and will get back up again. Another day to bob, weave, duck, swerve, jab, cross, upper-cut, move back and forth, from side to side. He needed to know when to pick his problems and when to keep quiet, and right now he needed time to think. Jake said, "Hey Jimmy, what nonsense—you almost done with the questionnaire?" Jimmy said, "I'm at the end of it, by the way, one is low, five is high right?" Jake said, "hmm, I think you might have flipped the scale." All Jake heard was a 'damn it.' Jimmy said, "Maybe I live under the influence of wishful thinking, but will things ever get better Jake? I knew it wasn't going to be easy, but I never thought it was going to be this hard. I always hear 'eventually, eventually'...well, eventually everyone grows old and dies."

Jake said, "Listen old friend, wishful thinking can be good, just fill the survey out and quit listening to me too much, before I turn you paranoid like myself. Every step forward is a step away from the past. I'm gonna take off."

What was he thinking? 'Every step forward is a step away from the past?' He was starting to sound like a shoe-shining leech that'd given him backlash day and night; here he was giving the same typical response to Jimmy. Jake smelled someone near him. Sardeep? It was Sardeep. Jake had an impeccable sense of smell, and Sardeep had an inimitable scent. Jake said, "What are you doing around here Sardeep?" Sardeep responded, "Nothing much, Jake, just want you to know, I'm on your team, we are all one and the same." Jake smirked at this, "Yup, sure." Sardeep said, "Also, well, I was talking to Ari and then....." Sardeep stopped in his delivery while his pad lit up with what looked like a message, "Jake! Oh, project junior lead. Look, my pad, Yes! Yes!" Sardeep moved away quickly, eager to begin work on his new project. Jake was flummoxed at such eagerness and loyalty, and for only a junior lead position? Sardeep probably didn't even finish the message in his eagerness and pride in his small elevation. Boxes-On-Top thrived on the Sardeeps and Aris of the world. Boxes-On-Top sensed their need for validation, their fragile loyalties, and their thirst for any recognition. They would feed them the occasional projects, the occasional commissions, and keep the employees divided.

This self-hating behavior was disappointing in his colleagues. Sardeep and Ari only provided the friction of teamwork, where the only other forces of work physics was pushing work sheets around. BLC, like any company, cared more about reputation and ego over product. Hidden within language and mottos like "client first" was the understanding that it meant the client would be first to be sacrificed, followed by the employee. Jake needed a walk and wandered through some of the various rooms in the office. They were filled with faux trees, and faux nature, surely another lab invention to give the impression of nature where there was really just dim lighting and narrow office ways. HR was even inserting sleep pods into the office. All these gadgets they'd place in the office to mimic a more natural setting. Nothing was sacred. All kinds of gadgets, surveillance equipment and products failed to produce the 'optimal' environment and ended up being an empty echo of the real one. What was behind it all of course was a constant search for maximum economizing. These sleep pods weren't about sleep; they were about the cost of fatigue.

Jake's sense of hearing wasn't nearly as good as his sense of smell, but he heard some commotion nearby and wanted to walk away. He'd heard the conversation through the newly built corner office being prepared for a Box-On-Top. BLC really picked the cheapest walls and put this room right against a new meeting room. Jake didn't want to hear the conversation, but couldn't help listening in, even though it was slightly fragmented. "I skip work … Fridays …because…" "That damn employee … I touched them…" "You ever … tired of the … now let me tell you…" The voices were all different. Jake couldn't discern who it was, but certainly he could hear, "Box-On-Top...Box-On-Top...being a Box-On-Top," and multiple other references—must have been some manager meeting. Wait… I do …couldn't be…yeah—it was HR in there as well! All right hit the jackpot there. What could they be meeting about and how could some of those phrases even be coming out? "…saying I touch them…"

What could that be? Although Jake had superior olfaction and could detect all sorts of smells (the over-microwaved foods odorating their rank fumes, the excessively perfumed colleague, the stale air) it was his sense of hearing that would pull him into trouble or pain, because he could hear the stupidity of the coworkers on the aisle and up to two aisles down discussing the nonsense of a burger and soda versus a double patty burger and no soda, or something else mundane. Jake kept listening, "Well,—all he had to do was focus a bit." Jake thought, *who's he*? The what of the conversation seemed less important than the "who." Jake kept listening, "So I might have touched the employee, but is that really wrong?" HR or what sounded like HR responded, "No, no, it's okay, talk about it, and it'll all be okay, this is the purpose of these sorts of things. We are here so all of you Boxes-On-Top can express yourselves." Jake was uncomfortably curious. More voices, "My turn? So, there was this one time, I asked the employee if they had any extra time? That employee told me no. I laid in and barreled into them." Some other voice responded, "Oh, quite interesting, I had something similar happen. I don't ask, or I do, but I say, 'you have enough work?' and it's rhetorical, because I just assign more anyway." What must have been HR said, "Good, good, we all know it's difficult sometimes, but just remember, we are here for the productivity of BLC."

Another voice chimed in, "They mean nothing. We determine nothing. We are heading in that direction but aren't there yet." And yet another voice said, "Just keep e-mailing them, if they don't respond, ask them if they got the first e-mail, then message them, call them, ..." Some voice said, "So on a different note, I've been told that I can be inappropriate, that some species can be more introverted—but you know it's just the way they are, that some of the females are known for, you know, well where do I start..." Must have been HR again responding, well, likely them responding, "Yes, let's be careful—what you're saying is dangerous." Jake thought with outrage, *this, this, is correcting bad behavior*? Jimmy waved at Jake through the window in the room. Jake waved him in. Jimmy said, "Jake, what are you doing in the room. There's no meeting." Jake said, "Listen Jimmy." Jimmy confused, "Listen to what?" Jake thought, *Jimmy's hearing must not be that great.*

"Well, I'll give you a bit of the summary. First, you probably don't want to hear it. Second, it's probably not a surprise anyway. Third, we've got to be quiet. Jimmy, whatever I heard just shows a broken escalation chain, and rule of corporate law." Jimmy was confused still, so responded "Uhm, yeah." Jake continued, "Sounds like someone's being harassed, sounds like a lot of bullying, and it's all forgiven. But imagine *your* mistake Jimmy; get a number wrong, or make the same mistake as a Box-On-Top, not that you would even be close to some of those types of mistakes. You'd get thorough punishment and would be retrained." Jimmy responded, "Jake, this is downright sad." Jake said, "Sad and real. Never thought that these kinds of things would be looked on as redeemable, correctable, group work sessions. Imagine if employees gathered in this type of union or way. These unions would be broken, and although these Boxes-On-Top are accessories to ethical breakages, it seems that 'group confessions' are ok for them, just not for us. Instead of correcting the mistake, these meetings take the place of punishment and instead offer solace. HR actually sounded like they were helping them, at best to look the other way, and at worst, to train themselves on how to mask their illegitimate acts.

Jimmy said, "I don't know what to say, does that mean if there's an issue we don't report it?" Jake said, "Well, doesn't seem to make a difference. Who knows? It might even mean we get in trouble instead." Jimmy said, "Eh, really, we would get in trouble?" Jake, said, "I don't know, seems like knowing the wrong information or people, and nowadays, reporting the wrong thing probably just gains you nothing—let's just put it like that." Jake finished his statement right as Zach was approaching. Jake said, "Zach, tell me you didn't hear any of this?" Zach said, "Sure, sure I did. What do I do to keep my mouth closed and this a secret?" Jake said, "Shove…" Zach cut him-off, "Hey, be careful there with any planned insults. You have 3 seconds." Jake assumed it was a bluff, "Yes, so I took extra snacks." Zach said, "Wait, that's it?" Jake said, "Yes." Zach said, "Jimmy involved?" Jake responded, "No." Zach pressed on, "Well, still bad, but might not be reportable immediately. Consider me an 'imperfect ally' Jake." Jake said, "'Ally' might not be the word. Jimmy, let's go." They both left the area. All it took was a slight mis-statement to get investigated—that is, if you fit the right profile, i.e. you weren't someone's relative or didn't remind someone of themselves as a little chick, pup, or whatever, because in those cases some clemency might be gained.

Jake was at his desk, reading various notes flooding in. This had to take the howl to the moon award it was so obvious that it was a pandering memo; it was from a visiting Chief Executioner Officiant to BLC Corp. CEO (as it was more commonly abbreviated) was as high as you could get in terms of being a Box-On-Top. You had tremendous corporate power. You would officiate over all manner of projects and budgets, and you could issue truth. Your general selection was a matter of nepotism and occasionally a rise from the bottom (so occasional it might as well be errata in a company's history). The CEO from earlier had sent this memo around:

> "*Make your work and your passion one and the same and do it with creatures you want to be with. Work is either 1) what you do to earn the units (i.e. money) to pay for the life you want or 2) what you do to achieve the corporate mission, or some mix of the above. Do that and everything will go better than if you don't.*"

What a wonderful, obvious and understanding statement. If you are starving, eat. If you are poor, get rich. If you don't like your job, try to like it, or find one that is likeable, and people who you want to spend time with, spend time with them, making mostly unnecessary products, and creating unnecessary marketing ...and....yeah. Jake wanted to immediately delete the note, but he let it sit there. He yelled "Hey Jimmy, you see the note from the visiting CEO?" Jimmy responded, "We've had a long enough day Jake, surveys, that awful conversation we were overhearing and now this, I need a break friend." Jimmy, poor, Jimmy, gullible until the end. Jake would never find someone like Billy to talk to. Darn. 11:42:10...he was 12 minutes and 10 seconds late to the next meeting. It was about budgeting for the next 3 and 5 years out. It was kind of crazy how companies planned their employees' entire lives, so to speak, and gave themselves only the utmost care and thought. Jake hadn't planned past the next day what he'd eat, and he was doubtful that any other employee took that much care in his or her own life. It felt like a bit of a sacrificial stupidity to look out for the firm first. "Do unto thyself, before onto others" should have been placed somewhere in the corporate commandments. Jake chuckled to himself. Tomorrow he'd plan how much of the game he'd play at least!

Chapter 22:
Out Sick (Quiet Interlude)

Anxiety. Stomach cramping. Muscles knotting up. Sweat pouring in. Teeth grinding. Could he? What would everyone think—that he wasn't able to work, that he was skipping. If only he could turn off or pause the imagined stream of opinions. Sardeep would say, "I knew it, always calling in sick, you know he's been sick 3 days in 5 years?" Ari would retort, "Probably trying to find another job," Hassan would chime in, "He's free!" and get everyone in trouble, Jimmy would weep, Cluster, would echo in some judgment, Rachel, and everyone else another. That is how Jake speculated it would go. But Jake thought too much and struggled to not care. I mean, he really did feel sick—sick of work—and mental health mattered right? The stress of hitting the 'send' button on his arm pad was enough to cause him to feel ill. Jake decided to voice it in instead 'send sick code #49209 to department.' Jake officially reported in ill. Maybe he'd a play a game on his pad, but of course, the damn pad seemed inoperative. It just worked a minute ago to send the sick code out. Hmm, this was rare but maybe useful?

The pad provided games, and other conveniences, but also tracked some work progress, location and other items that were less appealing. He lounged around, thinking *what next*? No time to procrastinate today. Look what happened to Billy. They might find more items in Billy's room and start going through all the connections: him, Jimmy, Geraldine. Having nothing isn't a sin or shame...but knowing nothing, doing nothing, that must be. Peer pressure, marketing and society were quite the judge of even knowledge (good to know about the newest products, fashion trends, and gadgets, but don't dare study existence) and action (don't skip work, but everything else was optional). Jake always wondered how Stephan, the old decrepit slothful creature, felt—he lived at the bottom of Building 41-604-13-4-13. Stephan wandered around the lower levels of the street. He kicked around the air and then ran back to jump to his tube. He was an odd fellow, found to be unfit for corporate work. He was a rare individual in that he lived outside of the world of work and whatever scraps in the disposal units that he found were his treasures to meals. He was grandfathered into the building's tenancy and there must have been a bug in the code that allowed him to live there for so long, particularly with his lack of employment and lack of corporate servitude. Lot of odd fellows in this decrepit building, maybe Jake was odd too? That house had become a second coat of their existence. Covered by their beliefs, then their bodies and their loved ones (or a lack thereof), and finally by this container giving them shelter, if nothing else.

His mind wandered. It was so easy to get distracted because there were so many things to distract, and these distractions were easy: easy to access, to load up on, cheap in a sense. There was media, gadgets, trinkets, and more. The most popular media was video channels, search channels, story channels, any channel you could want. The brain really had one path with media, to sink low and glide down into that lazy zombified path. Imagination was sapped, and the creature sedated, and all was at peace and social harmony. The small guise of free will to choose your media, choose your vice and addiction and then to lose yourself, and the irony was that you'd pay to rob yourself with your time, identity or morality.

Information and theories were available more than imaginable (of course after corporate historians removed the unsavory bits, to the point where even they couldn't remember the unsavory bits), but creatures were not the intelligent, understanding, or capable creatures they used to be. How could you expect the corporate drone, exhausted, bent, and broken, to have the energy or care to explore past their basic sustenance? Their bubble was safe enough. If someone died, and they were outside of your bubble, you didn't care. After all, only your own death would nudge you to some feeling.

Not everything was the corporation's fault. Power does not always corrupt; the individual often arrives corrupt, looking for power to magnify them, and the power they seek is merely the vessel. To some it was responsibility and honor. The unselfish nature of those who sought power for responsibility and honor allowed the corruption to take power and make it concrete. There were also trinkets and gadgets galore, silly things multiplied many times over, while what was important shrank. The only consistent thing was everything commercial, and what was cheap was 'easier' and more convenient. At what cost came convenience?

Take food, for example. When food was varied, organic, and difficult to obtain it was also a point of pleasure, a way to feel hunger, and satisfy that hunger. True, deep, unadulterated hunger creates a pain that only its satiation resolves. Hunger did not exist without food being the object of consumption, and food needed hunger. Food itself also never had evil intentions; you never traded your soul for a bag of chips (and really, what are chips other than tasty salty morsels of fried fats?). It was more than food; it created a platform for social gathering, from organized lunches to group outings. Food added greater satisfaction to any event. To not know a pain is to not know a pleasure. With the installation of feeding tubes decades ago in home and the place of productivity, organic creatures had to traverse only between two destinations, cutting out the social lines created and removing the natural distraction, the feeling of hunger and satisfying that hunger. Hunting, whether via chasing down an animal or moving down shopping aisles, was extinct. The feeding tubes had embedded sensors and released the necessary amount of nutrients into the body. Order in the world maintained, resources and quotas kept measured. Yet the various experience, research and trials indicated otherwise, since even the feeding tubes couldn't free organic creatures of their need for interaction. The generations raised on feeding tubes, of course had forgotten anything before their existence.

Jake grabbed the "book" with the folded map and started looking at its drawings. On the paper was a bunch of arrows on the old streets, pointing to a defunct area nearby. There were many once-decrepit cities on the way to becoming corporate mega cities. The urbanized areas were mostly shrunk, transformed to farmland, experimental water plantations and other oddities. Jake was going to start exploring this map. He had to—he didn't know when he'd get the chance again. He started flipping through the book—it had so many words!!! He was getting dizzy. The attention span required for work was very different than that of free reading. The book felt magical. Jake immediately felt his emotions enlarge. He was seeing and understanding and learning. He had to go to this library, find more of these books. He grabbed his one work bag, emptied it, and filled it with water and some snacks he'd surreptitiously snuck out of the office. He quickly checked his pad, but it still looked inoperable. Good. No tracking. He immediately went to the archaic elevator shaft; he still knew how to operate it.

He bumped into Stephan, who looked surprised, "Jake. What are you doing here?" Jake said, "Oh, just going to go down and get this pad fixed." Stephan was confused, "Where would you get that fixed? You don't go down to get that fixed? Go to the office Jake, they'll fix it." Jake said "Yeah, good idea Stephan." He didn't want to get caught up in a chat that would not end well. Stephan faced towards Jake while he was moving away, "Yeah, I think Billy's was broken as well." Jake thought, *how did he know Billy?* Jake wanted to ask but thought it more prudent to leave the subject alone. A few folks knew Billy. Jake wandered around the street, keeping his eyes high, looking over his shoulder. There was the usual fog of heavy pollution overhead and some drones buzzing around, but it was rare for anyone to go out into the old streets and it didn't look like the drones paid him any attention. Must be the broken pad?

Jake was getting lost—none of these streets, nor old buildings looked livable. He moved from one street to the next. There was a large broken hunk of metal. It looked hollow. Four wheels, four view screens or something electronic, and perhaps couches inside? Must have been some archaic transportation device, he was guessing. The wheels gave it away. There were some wires strewn near it. Some old dusted bags. Jake was tempted to open a bag. He started walking away and then turned back. A few minutes of checking and exploring wouldn't hurt. PTWSD, Post-Traumatic Work Stress Disorder, hit him and he froze. What if Cluster popped out and grabbed him. Eddie, Kevin, Calistis. Someone will know. They must have tracked him by now. He would be humiliated. He had to stop these thoughts. Let him get back to this wondrous adventure. "Jake, just stop, no consequences, no risk, no reward, search!" he commanded himself.

He grabbed a bag and started opening it slowly. He thought, *hmm, maybe I should hide in that metal hunk.* He grabbed what looked like an opening and swung what appeared to be a door. He pulled into the vehicle, and dragged the semi heavy bag in. He pulled out what looked like little figurines.

What was the purpose of these? Some ancient idols or toys? He found an archaic electronic device with a digital screen. It made him laugh. Primitive. A device should be so integrated into you that you and the device are one. This device looked like you could disconnect from it. He found some cylinders. Pictures of what looked like meat and vegetables. Jakes pad started to blink on again!!! Uh oh. Jake dropped the bag quickly and thought. Should I run back? If I'm detected outside of the building or the office I will be in serious trouble. The lights went back off. Jake started going towards the arrows on all paws outside. One arrow was smudged. Hmm. Right, or left? Go right. Jake saw a large marble engraving on top of what appeared to be a wooden door. He entered an abandoned building. It was the library.

He found still images with burned edges. Individuals with silly hats and sillier awkward poses. There were some where they were standing by themselves. He found old, broken devices that looked like they might have even been from the Age of Tabulated Phones of Smarts (and before that the Age of Big Box TV's and Commercials). It was funny because digital illness wasn't instant but crept in with every innovation One didn't carry a big box TV it seemed, but at some point they shrunk that TV, put in a computer and then plugged in an eye scanner…and then…yeah, lots of things developed after that. After predictions became realities and world population grew to uncountable numbers, the production of food became more about minimal sustenance, measured quantities, and rations. There were wars, famines and reformations until the Corporate Age came along and brought some measure of peace. Technological improvements incremented a thousand times to the point where one created surplus. The ability to transform the gifts of silicon to simulate their worlds via machines and circuits became a reality. Self-driving cars, self-walking feet, and all manner of other inventions followed.

Jake continued, looking through the library. There were tags on some of the tablets, 'Celebrity Reviewed, Rich endorsed, Expert recommended...' The obsession with celebrities must have been fiendish to use up all that digital storage for photos of mutated and cartoonish characters. There was a section of printed colored papers made of some plastic material. They showcased home products, child products, adult products, hair...teeth...if the marketing department could see the history, maybe it was better that these things were buried behind this door.

Jake discovered a section that consisted exclusively of books (no old tablets or anything) called 'Photography' and he stopped to take a look. Photos of families spending time together. Photos of scientific discoveries. There were books on beliefs. It was interesting how much he'd read in other books, journals, and publications how the creatures would protest beliefs because they could not see them, of miracles they could not touch, of prophets they could not see, to texts espousing good that they could not practice. They could not accept the multi-pronged dimensionality of practice, nor the simple acceptance of belief, and even if they could accept the belief itself, the idea that this belief took work, that they had to practice it seemed too laborious. It was idealistic belief versus practice of belief. The corporations did not promise a hell or heaven, long awaited, but immediately delivered micro-hells, micro-payments and so on. Fear would wane with the patience of believers, and employees were numb to only the immediate feelings of being yelled at, removed from their employment, or pushed into menial tasks. The nature of creatures perhaps, was that they felt only things that threatened them in the present, and these took priority, but not the larger risks, mistakes, or lack of awareness of their existence. Arguably the greatest characteristic a believer needed was a belief tempered by resilience and patience.

Interestingly, the politicians and the owners were nothing but corrupted individuals and were happy to take, guide, or save the employees, consume them with fear, and get them to produce with very restrictive purpose. God did not need creatures, but creatures needed God. God could create the entirety of existence, yet neither fear nor love drove the believers to God. *How interesting,* thought Jake. Perhaps creatures even corrupted religion? So many messages, yet the only messages creatures listened to were in email form, a stern email, or demotion, and that punishment seemed so much more real because it came from another creature. The corporate prophets believed in themselves and took the assets of others and their beliefs unto themselves. Most humble and ordinary creatures, while quick to reproach their fellow employees, or the weak, were slow and incapable of making the same leaps against the systems that used them.

Jake felt the hours pass by slowly. His pad still showed the time. He had only been there for a few hours, but it felt liberating. If only he could bring some of these things to life, or enter through some portal, stretch away the current time and dive back into that previous era.

It looked like the species had reached the fulcrum of accomplishment through corporate momentum and corrupt officials, and all that this required was the consent of the sheepish and numbed populace to create this world. There could have been many alternative worlds, but this was the one that was created. Jake could remember being in the office more than any other activity. Jake remembered work, more than family, more than love, more than friends, more than stories. Typing and voicing into pads, not playing in parks. Spreadsheets, robotic arms, and filling out forms, not raising a brood or sitting in the open, just enjoying beauty or smelling fresh air. Learning about the corporate rules, commandments, not reading history, or forming the future. An employee was part of history and the owners determined the future. He walked down an aisle where there were quirky looking screens with what appeared to be one button. He clicked it, and following a whirling sound, the power went on. Jake saw a menu of touch screen items. He blew away a bit of the dust and started scrolling through the menu. He watched a few self-made seemingly amateur videos on random topics.

Apparently, these were captured in siloed experiences and sent through tabular devices to the point where no one needed to see anyone anymore. If you could send a picture, why see them? If you could text them, why talk to them? If you could wear it, consume it, why shouldn't you? Surely all this separation set the foundation that must have contributed to the corporate takeovers, divided even to the point where families (as he'd learned in a separate book), became non-existent. Individuals occasionally gathered for procreation, eating frozen yogurts and drinking kofeie, cofes, coffees...whatever... it was a wonder the species didn't inadvertently destroy itself. What was clear was the lack of care, from creation and innovation by the species.

He moved on. He saw an aisle on politics. He was trying to learn and interpret. Political evolution. Emperors. Dictators. Democracy, Kleptocracy, Socialocrasy, Capitalism, Socialism, Favoritism...vote the rich back in, create your own dictators, mix and match your fools. Nations said they were built on thoughts and ideals but really they were built on the backs of natives, backs of slaves, backs of poor and speciesism. What was speciesism? The assignment of different values, rights, or special consideration to individuals solely on the basis of their species! Innocence was on a sliding scale; some nations raped, and pillaged, others were works in progress. There were so many more ways to die—nuclear war and disease—that old age seemed to be the exception at some point.

The politics of old make you realize how simple the politics of today are, or at least the way they seemed simple. The elite, in power, the lobbyist, the laziness all mixed in, and the few willing to decide, or intelligent enough to decide and then those who forced decisions. Networks were only owned by a few names, media channels, companies, land, utilities, you name it. And interestingly every time it seemed things changed, it became apparent the species just reinvented the same concept in a new way with slight loosening of freedoms here and there while tightening things elsewhere. Power mongers, despots whether in religion, government, or corporations would slosh back and forth, borrowing from each other, distributing freedom and pushing fear, all while feasting on work and collective distribution. An individual felt alone even though 99% of the world was doing the same thing they were, and 1% owned the rest of them.

Jake had enough, he moved on. He checked an aisle on foods, then dieting, then economics. The one on nutrition/ketogenics/bsgeneics, etcetera, was interesting; some groups stopped eating, just to have smaller hind ends, some ate more to have bigger hind ends—the amount of time spent on body sculpting while half the planet was dying without choice of carb or protein was astonishing. Maybe there were worse times than the Corporate Age (as Jake called the present). Interesting, apparently 90% of the world population appeared to suffer, whereas 9% subsided and 1% excelled. Maybe it was a function of the species that most individuals were average, and only a small portion should succeed. The more likely explanation was that nepotism, and the lack of movement by those oppressed caused those in power to grow into certainty, and to thrive there—fattened on their tablets, seeing themselves as superior to the other 90% of the world, devoid of any morals or values. If they could see us now, we all share in the same mediocrity. The shame is that most of the pain inflicted was by the species itself, not by nature, or space invaders or anything external. But by the corporate masters and their agreeable groups, thinking themselves superior.

They assumed some biological difference made them superior, some religious view, some history (and assumed that all of the previous was revisable to fit their future). Something as simple as the founding of nations, of apartheid states, military juntas, colonialist juggernauts, became cereal factories, shirt production lines, and energy-producing entities. The irony of it all was the hypocrisy—the founders not allowing their own broods to use their own products or government officials not sending their own to sacrifice for their wars, or the attitude towards foreigners while being foreign themselves. One day someone was a God, the next, no more. One day something doubled your life, the next day it ended it. One day a war was the only way, the next it appeared not so. The media had excelled in numbing them, comforting them, and most of all distracting them.

Jake found some scrolls. Or, wrapped up…picture galleries, hmm, picture books maybe. They had these characters shooting out energy from their appendages, some wearing capes, and well, just odd things. Must have been to sell toys and indoctrinate, or maybe for fun—hopefully these creatures weren't real. Imagine anyone being able to shoot blasts of energy through their paws, claws, wings or appendages? Who knows. It might have even been a distraction like the many distractions he read about—movies, videos—whilst the corporations grew and grew. He saw something that wasn't this collection of papers, but a device. It took him a while to figure out how to operate it, not because of its sophistication, its multipronged handles, buttons and options. Ironically because of its simplicity. One button? Had to be some sort of deadly weapon or tracking device, or creatures than couldn't contemplate past on/offs, swipes, or switches.

He took a deep breath, ran around and howled, then said his last prayer, and hit the button. A blast of audio waves of various fragments, singing a colloquial tune rang out. He waited three minutes, and 15 seconds later guttural language arose, but what a sound, what a beat! Jake smiled, oh what a device. Ancient, but producing this beautiful sound! He would take it with him and would play on tube rides home or sneak away somewhere to play it. Who was going to hear, the tube operator? His colleagues? The world? He was excited about this gadget. The tube was one of the only physical constructs that reminded one there was some existence outside of the building of work or corporate home. One needed it to transport from the corporate home to the place of rest. These conduits zigzagged across the city and amazingly everything intersected and moved almost instantly with no interruptions or crashes. Well almost no crashes. There was the incident were wiring had routing issues and sent too many individuals packetized down the wrong tube, so the cracked tubes had to be replaced. Well, some audio waves sure would have made it all better.

Jake was ready to leave. He was walking towards the back when he fell over a book. Backsliding, he grabbed it— *Autobiography of Malcolm X*, the title read. He flipped through to the end. Interesting…he had to take this book with him. It was tagged under classics…he started wandering the aisles quickly. He had to find this aisle. There were books on things called, 'poetry,' 'design,' 'Aesops Fables,' and all sorts of books. He would have to come back to learn more. He tucked his newfound treasure, *Autobiography of Malcolm X*, in the small pack he brought. His time was almost up, and he had to return.

He walked back towards the towers. The conduits zigzagged across the city. Tubes took you from home pod to the

Place of Productivity and Innovation (also known as work). Amazingly everything intersected and moved almost instantly with no interruptions or crashes. But really it made no difference now. The dread of going back was now supported by the reality of how empty it all was.

Chapter 23:
yftp://YogaForThePeople

Easing back into the office Jake signed up for a team activity—yoga. He was reading over the list of attendees: the 800-pound gorilla (let's see him bend over and touch his toes), the cash cows (someone always trying to scam them), red herrings (sending everyone in the wrong direction), war hawks (enough said), fat cats (was it wrong to eat too many snacks?), and even lame ducks (lame was in the eye of the beholder). Jake walked into the room and the elephant was there as well. The corporate face would take the form of an ass, donkey, or bird, and would break its many creatures in this yoga studio into seekers of the ancient stretching arts. It gathered those more prone to meditation, and groupthink forces were in full effect. What was Jake to do in the face of irrational exuberance? Well, join in, to "be rational was to be irrational" (or at least that's what was being chanted as instruction while everyone gathered next to each other in the room). Jake leaned over and started asking the creature next to him, "Silly question, but…" All he got was a response of "shhh" from various angels, followed by a single voice, "give him a silly answer."

Jake thought, *forget it*. The lights were coming off. A culture of instant gratification, say fast food, lighting fast food, instant food yearned for something slow, and what slower than empty meditation to fit the bill? Jake tried imitating the humming, "uhmmmmmm." He started falling asleep as his mind wandered. The chant continued, "We are oneeee. We are oneeee." Jake struggled, "I am, we are, uhmmmmm." Mental barriers were being eroded, self-protective and self-identifying thoughts disappearing (better for you to have your time than someone else, better for you to come to a conclusion than be forced to one), and if these core values were so malleable they must not have been core enough, or perhaps the forces against them too powerful. Or maybe Jake was confusing core-vales with "uhmmmmm." Jake continued, "uhmmmmm." The group chant continued, "Life has no limits. Life has no limits." Jake hadn't done much yoga, or any really, but semi-consciously muttered, "…but it sure has boundaries." Fear would do what force would have done but Jake's fear of not fitting in wasn't strong enough to counter the force of a dying dog stretch. He rolled into a squat pose and fell asleep. A heavy force nudged him and the sound of "uhmmmmm" was humming through the room. It was getting quite humid. Jake got up, stepping on a few tentacles, hooves, and other unlucky appendages as he walked out of the studio.

In the room next door, there was a farmer's market, bull market, bear market and dog-and-pony show. Lots going on today in the office building aside from yoga studio: arts and crafts, work-on-lunch programs, long list. The ducks were all in a row waiting to get into that market with a sacred cow or two behind them (distant cousins of the cash cow). There were some fish out of water, a nest of vipers, cold turkeys sitting near a broken temperature control. There was a kangaroo court and tail-wagging dogs. Night owls, flies on the wall and ducks and drakes loitering, what was that event? Jake just couldn't take the euphemism, metaphor, analogy, and soliloquy anymore.

As distracting as yoga at work was Jake felt he was still somehow being beguiled and robbed. The corporation attempted efficient robbery. Your future was payable upon completion of your indentured servitude, education stalled, health collateralized—a thief at least had the decency to rob you only your material possessions. To move beyond this would mean to remove yourself from that environment, and that was impossible. The social hook snapped into the flesh of the heart, and wormed its way into the mind. The social order was too strong, and a lifetime of rejection and seeking acceptance slamming you back and forth kept one from progressing. Maybe Jake was looking at it the wrong way, but what other way was there to look at it without being deceitful to the situation? Who knows which came first, perception, facts, or nonsense? Plus, they had a yoga studio now. Trying to find happiness from work is like trying to buy truth serum from a politician. Jake uhmmmmm'd to himself, but it didn't seem to work without the group chant.

If a corporation was consistent about anything it was hypocrisy. At least most governments faded (from what he read in the library. They use to be prominent, large, full of frightful creatures using intelligence and power not to serve but to rule, or sell power to the highest bidder). Government consent and indebtedness to the corporation left government will to corporate mercy and allowed organizational evolution to culminate in corporations supplementing government. At least the corporations were efficient at cruelty and hypocrisy and could take the mantle of rule and mutate it. Yoga time again, Jake might have been thinking too much, uhmmmmm, and decided to do some wandering.

There was a portrait of Quinn near the outside of the yoga studio. Scraped and old, his face had a white stripe extending down his orange frame, a comedic smile and head enclosed in a spherical apparatus containing water. "Click, Cluck, Clicheee" was written in some gibberish scratched into the portrait. Must have been graffiti. Under that etching read,

"Living the dream…" Quinn was a pitiful soul to some (to Jake, for example) and a hero to most (everyone else). He was not a Zach, a Tse, a Cluster, not intent on lying or bred to be conniving, but he fell towards those qualities until they became habit.

He wasn't in his natural setting in the culture of business, of automatically consuming profits, costs, turnovers, risks in their quantities, or applications but he did believe business made an individual more accountable than an individual in their natural state. He dreamed but stopped imagining. He was managed but never led. He completed work but was never productive (who was?). He was layered in by Boxes-On-Top, who were harvesting him for work. He was one to never spend wildly, he would say "units come and go" (mostly go of course), but "we only get one soul…dedicate it to the company and it will pay off in retirement, accolades, and accomplishments." Quinn would hold staring matches with other employees for fun. An odd follow, but an ideal employee. He kept a summarized version of the commandments in his desk, "Quinn's shorthand":

1. The corporation is always right
2. The corporation is for the people, lest the people are in the way of the corporation
3. Competence is incompetence, and incompetence is competence

He had patented a few work tactics, stating the obvious and making awkward moments more awkward. Boxes-On-Top, HR, owners, nepotistic colleagues, failed co-employees, the whole lot. They wanted you to care whether they did or not; they were vain, hypocritical and jealous to say the least (to say the most would be too much for writing). At the same time, they were nobody. But to Quinn, they were his existence. And the tragedy of it all is that none of it paid—in units, recognition past the walls of a building or in health and happiness. 40 years for the corporation, completing vesting and nothing to show for it. In and out quickly. Quinn was forgotten. It was just the portrait. Jake should have wandered farther.

Chapter 24:
Uniq-corn The Dream Manager

Billy was marched in front of everyone in a fit of final public humiliation. HR said, "Billy...?" Billy wouldn't make eye contact with Jake or anyone else. It appeared as if he were looking at a screen. Billy said, "All—thank you to the corporation, I am on my way to retirement." There were a few coughs, yaws, and whispers of '*aww*.' Some were sincere, and some were less so. Billy looked toward Jake for a brief second; it looked like the glimmer of a nod. Jake thought Billy must have either been brainwashed or was attempting to limit the damage and prevent his friends from being hurt. Billy would never agree to such public humiliation. They could have offered him something, perhaps even some form of immunity. Billy continued, "I have made some mistakes, and they are all on my own, but I do own them. I am grateful for all the time with BLC, for the training, and the mentorship. BLC takes you and gives you purpose in life. We make the best products, provide the best services, and guarantee the best warranty. And most of all, BLC shows the best support to its wor—" Billy paused, seemingly in thought. He looked at Jake. Jake wanted to say, "Do what you want Billy. Your dignity isn't worth this. Don't sacrifice your dignity."

Behind Billy loomed a new figure. He had a singular horn and well-maintained mane. He had to be new, a fresh Box-

On-Top. HR almost encircled poor Billy aside from the small opening for the audience to see him. Billy finished, "The great travesty is that, the great travesty is that..." Jake wanted to raise his hand and yell, "Stop! The great travesty is the enormous disregard for the CEO curtain that we all sit here and blatantly ignore!" But courage withdrew, and logic stepped in. If Billy had sacrificed himself, what would Jake's outburst gain? What if Billy didn't, and he needed that one shout? What if...

Billy continued, "...the great travesty, is that I don't get to work at BLC any longer. I am looking forward to retirement to reminisce about my years at BLC, maybe travel a bit between the corporate sanctioned retirement corral nearby." HR nodded at each other, and then Billy ended it with "Well, one more thing. The future belongs to those who prepare for it today." HR was confused; they motioned to someone. 'Check the screens' was inadvertently held over the speaker. Jake thought this must be a message. Billy must have gone off script; it was his "goodbye" to his friend. HR said, "Ok get back to work everyone."

Jake might have been back at the office, but things had changed. He could never go back mentally. Who could he talk to? What next? How would he survive? His thoughts were rapidly firing. Sardeep ran over, "We have a new Box-On-Top." Lou echoed him excitedly, "Yes, indeed, they say he is a true leader!" Management was working on training and leadership programs. Uniq-corn was the great facilitator. He could convince and move anyone it was said. Uniq-corn walked out. Sharp. White. Uniq-corn. Well-spoken. He apparently was raised somewhere in the Northern lands. There was something a bit odd about him as well. He'd heard Jake might need inspiration. He started speaking to some folks on the way and walked over to Jake, "Jake, you have a minute?" *Seemed more put together than Tse, Cluster, and the rest*, thought Jake. Jake responded,

"Certainly." Uniq-corn took Jake for a walk and said, "Listen we want you to step up." Jake said, "Uhm, you mean work harder and put in more hours?" Uniq-corn said, "Sure, you can call it what you want Jake, but we really are going to help you achieve." Jake found Uniq-corn strangely competent and in that sense dangerous, "Yes, I will." Uniq-corn continued, "I'd like us to meet every week." Jake asked, "Do I have a say in this?" He never would have said such a thing before, but things had changed. He'd seen worlds that existed and realities bigger than the rules of only this place. Uniq-corn responded, "Say in what?" He was trying to make Jake's confidence brittle. Jake responded, "In how often we meet?" Uniq-corn responded, "No, Jake. You do not have a say." Jake was disappointed.

Uniq-corn, in a fit of self-indulgence, called Jake back, "Hey Jake—come back here for a minute—you think you can come up with a better system? Why didn't you become a Box-On-Top, or a CEO? Why didn't you improve the world? Actually Jake, don't answer that." There was no point in responding. Jake thought, *Why didn't I become a Box-On-Top?* as if the system worked like that—as if the system was made by one being and not by multiple elites, colluding, monopolizing for centuries. "Sure," said Jake. "I can change the system—but would you allow it? Accept it? Is there a complete system?" *Of course, not,* Jake thought. "But there's a better existence than this. Also, you always have to call it a system, whatever that means to you. Constantly plugged in—constantly being messaged and messaging. Controlled and surrounded, lonely but never alone—never alone in the wrong way. The only thing one could indulge in was groveling and more work." Uniq-corn said, "War has rules and life has rules, but the only rule here is that of the strong. A manager has to be capable of anything." Jake thought, *what hyperbole.* Uniq-corn quipped, "You can't chase someone or something back into your paws Jake...Billy is

gone...don't think we haven't been monitoring everything here."
Jake thought *at least "here" means not the home; whatever was
left of it and his recent exploration.* Jake was sarcastic, "How
about we all lose hope, have nothing to look forward to. The
moment you stop imagining things is probably the best time as
an employee."

Uniq-corn was beyond a Cluster or Formange, or any of
the previous trained managers. He coolly responded, "Sure
Jake." Uniq-corn added, "You know why we know better, Jake?
You assume that managing is a cultured and culture-wide
activity, and not just individuals doing whatever they want. Of
course, we, Boxes-On-Top are held to greater accountability. We
have our own systems Even the incompetent Boxes-On-Top will
hold on for dear life, and the more destruction they apply the
more we will remove them. Well, save a few. You, you would
not be able to manage, lead, create, or produce. Lying, and
conniving is a skill just like any other. It requires practice. Build
the habit. Jake, I could have made you a Box-On-Top in a
different life, but frankly, it doesn't matter. You're too honest,
wear your heart on your sleeve and think too independently."
Jake coolly responded, "Sure." Uniq-corn smiled, "Companies
colonized Mars for the glory of all, and now we'll be shipping
resources from there and back, rather than a nation. It was called
privatization. Companies were less detectable. It is easier to hate
another nation. But to take that hate, and to shrink it back to
hating the person in the cubicle next to you, was easier because it
had less impact. Pit the individuals against each other as long as
they produce." Jake said, "You mean the virtually unchecked
corporation, for more than a few generations, will always rule?
Well, I'll tell you this, we can't say much more than a cycle of
consumption and production has taken place. No elevation of
morals, or of standards in art." Uniq-corn interrupted, "But how
do you want that funded? We need these markets of production."

Jake said, "It's rather the opposite. You need us to produce and consume, because who else truly generates the wealth to be gathered by the owners?" Everything went silent and Uniq-corn and Jake just stared at one another.

Chapter 25:
Good Things Happen to Bad Folks

Reorgs, HR training, new managers, work, work, work…then more work. Something bad had to happen to someone bad. Why? Well, because justice felt like it should be self-referential, free from the laws of physics, bribery, and any other laws. Really! That is if justice were just—some bad should happen to bad folks, just as good should happen to good folks, and not a lot in between. Simple. But the corporations managed to strip even justice naked, to mutilate it and finally mutate it. Jake didn't wish bad things in general; no one really did. It just seemed that only good things happened to bad people, and then by accident a good thing happened to a good person. That was just his perception.

Geraldine was nearby. Jake said, "Geraldine, how are you?" Geraldine responded, "To be honest…still a bit sad about Billy…I know you were close to him as well." Jake responded, "You just have to mask the pain, and show a different personality at work." Geraldine stared at Jake, surprised by his response, as she asked, "You okay Jake?" Jake laughed, "Oh, I am—I was joking—being gregarious or being grumpy around here accomplishes the same thing but at least the former adds to longevity. Anyway, guess who I was partnered with to improve my productivity recently?" Geraldine said, "Is Florian bothering you as well?" Jake responded, "Ah, not that groveling tool...Uniq-corn." Geraldine gasped, "I heard he's a bit of a monster. Smart AND capable, and calm on top of it all." Jake said, "Even worse. Just avoid him if you can." Geraldine, said, "How so?" Jake said, "Trust me, you don't want to know, he is worse than, say, a Cluster, he knows more, and is more intelligent. He is more polished and can get away with more. It's a matter of time before he moves up." Geraldine, said, "Well, as long as we avoid him I guess." Jake said to Geraldine, "We better march over to the award ceremony."

There wasn't always an awards ceremony, but one was coming up—what a great opportunity to watch the parade and show. Jake was a young pup once. He wasn't always the Jake of now; he wasn't always angry, unable to admit it, but possibly a bit bitter...he wasn't always resentful, but time and opportunity had passed. How many times was credit taken, not given? Memories and associated pain would return from a decade past, and of course, the recounting of that lost time and recounting of that lost opportunity could not be lamented enough. Those many moments compounded. His face scrunched, and his bowels felt irritated. Jake thought, *Am I doomed to never forget? Why can't I just let go, be happy, move on?* This was before the pain of Cluster, before this team, before Uniq-corn, and Florine; it was an older pain. He would sacrifice his time, work late, work early, work on everything. He would smile incessantly. He would talk and share everything, trust everyone. He still failed at that sometimes, as verbosity was a curse for him. His innocence was embarrassing.

Shame crept over Jake. He had no agenda and wanted to be loved as that young pup. To be recognized and told he was part of the team and to work on interesting stuff. Jake was truly more innocent once. There had been that manager who told him, "I will reduce your units to increase their units. Why? Because I want to." *The vindictiveness*, Jake thought. *To punish me, for being myself and speaking my mind. To reward that shriveled creature. Where was the justice? There was that one Shitzu—her cruelty in seating me next to her for monitoring. For speaking my mind. Where was the justice?"* he thought. There were the coworkers, feigning ignorance to collect information…and all of a sudden HR showing up. Where was the justice? Nowhere, that's where. For a time, he kept fighting himself instead of the system, reworking himself, when in reality, there wasn't any amount of work he could take upon himself to merge into the unjust environment. Maybe the system needed to be fought, and maybe it didn't, but the system encroached, cornered, and invaded the individual with it's agendas and uses for the employee.

There was no amount of groveling that was enough. Most folks did not care to know him, if any, past what he could do for them. Some of it was he was prejudged by—perhaps his breed, lineage, heritage, beliefs—there were all sorts of possible reasons. But really, who cared? Who cared what everyone wanted from him or thought of him? What he wanted for himself was what should have mattered. The problem was that one really never could think for themselves. *Really think.* These external pressures, these societal moldings, when misaimed would constantly push Jake into what they wanted him to be, or the only challenges given were the challenges that would shape him into who they wanted him to be. You "solve" the problem that you are given, but what if you could change the problem? The blessing was that his core self was unique. He knew himself at some point, at least. He hoped whatever he lost could be rebuilt in some way. It would never be the same, but in some way, Jake knew that his soul was well intentioned. That made sense to him, and that was good enough. Jake just wanted some of his innocence back.

The synthetic sound of horns and pre-recorded cheers were blaring. Jake snapped out of this mental race down memory lane. He was getting messaged by some colleague about a failed project. In relation to the company they were the employee, and in relation to each other they were colleagues. But one thing was certain: some of these aforementioned colleagues were incompetent. In an absolute sense, some of them were truly incompetent. The greater evil was the waste of time, the waste of one's existence. The irony, possibly, was this evil could be committed by the employee against themselves. They could waste their own time. Sure. They were incompetent in their own right. The greater evil of the system did not absolve the weak, the tired, and the outright ignorant. Being stupid was not a crime, but being ignorant was a choice, implicit or otherwise. Jake had to participate in such a meeting while running late to the office one day. He had that sound producing device in his pocket. He pulled it out, the music was blasting! Luckily the meeting was muted. Or it seemed muted. Good thing at least he muted himself before he called in. Imagine if he hadn't; they would have asked what this noise was, and it would have been over for him.

This mandatory award ceremony never felt like it would start, and then the lights went on. Kevin and Eddie walked by Jake with huge synchronized smirks, "You ready for your award Jake?" Sardeep and Lou were nearby, "Jake! You winning an award!?" They seemed jealous. Jake said, "Sardeep, Lou, you're going to believe Kevin and Eddie?" Jake thought, *forget it. Some people just don't get it.* Cluster and Tse were running behind Uniq-corn. Uniq-corn ignored Jake. Cluster and Tse, mimicking Uniq-corn, ignored Jake as well. HR had setup the auditorium and stage. HR said, "Greeeetingsssss everyone." There was a pause. Everyone responded back, "Salutations!" HR, echoed, "BLCCC, here we are, BLC, we are #1!" Sort of a funny statement, 'we are #1'—work was a fraudulent competition. In every case, the employee—the consumer—was bound to lose and the ultimate owners' (those above even HR and Boxes-On-Top)—were going to win. Their "competition" was just transference of power and wealth amongst each other. There was JCV, AEO, Blue Corps and more… the list went on, but they all merely transferred ownership amongst each other. There was one manager, Ferdion, who had one large fin and a glass, water-filled case around his gills with a machine attached. He was transferred recently as a Box-On-Top. The HR announcer called him to the stage, "Ferdion, come up here and help me hand out these awards." HR continued, "We'd like to call our first winner up. For the most committed employee, the award goes to Kevin." Eddie looked upset. Kevin ran up. Everyone else looked confused. Joey was furious. It didn't make sense. Jake also felt there was something shaky about his existence. What a mockery. Was he meant to toil and work for the same fate. To continue in the role of peon to the grand Box-On-Top? Perhaps. Then how was one to find salvation? What did *salvation* even mean? Retirement was around the corner, but is that what happens? One is to enjoy their life only once their bodies become decrepit and their life is post-work? That was one route, surely better than the latter. The other was more morbid.

The award ceremony continued. The prancing, dancing Committee of Entertainment moving around the stage and the room. Deep in the nature of every creature is the need for some form of recognition. This recognition in oneself is the most stable, safe, and necessary. The synthetic validation the corporation provided was subtle—in the occasional "Good job!" or random swag item, if even that. *Keep your "Good job!"* thought Jake. This foreign validation, only dressed in a cheap free-t shirt or an even cheaper set of words pieced together. Corporate recognition was backed by the value of the corporation; to some it was gold, to others, poison. Riding through biological circuitry were signals crossed with trained and elicited social habits that culminated in an emotional bombardment. Take two creatures and continuously reward one while explicitly or implicitly not rewarding the other. There are various resulting interactions that arise, and most of them are unsavory emotions.

Jake saw Geraldine again and walked back towards her. He said, "How are you? Anything change from 5 minutes ago?" Geraldine said, "Jake, do you need to ask?" Jake detected a more morose Geraldine and said, "Well my friend, I do care about how you are." Geraldine looked happier to hear this, "Thank you Jake." Jake pressed on, "So, how are you?" Geraldine, just said, "Tired Jake, tired." Jake knew the feeling. He responded, "You hear that joke Geraldine?" Geraldine looked around, "Jake, you are a trouble maker—no jokes, you know the rules. Jokes lead to stories, and rumors, and less productivity." Jake said, "Ok, forget the joke, but hear this: I'm thinking of moving on." Geraldine, confused, said, "What does *move on* mean?" Jake said, "Just stop coming." Geraldine laughed out loud, "You mean not show up for a day, unannounced, terminated, and then sent to training and eventually the Department of Lost Souls. You live in some messed up fantasy Jake. Quit imagining and day dreaming, and you'll be better off." Jake responded, "Perception is reality...but shouldn't be."

Murray was nearby, no eyes, a mouth full of razor sharp teeth, moving in agreement. Really he only had two motions, nodding yes or no seemed enough. At times it was amazing he was kept around. Jake asked, "How you doing Murray?" He knew fully well no response was going to be given, other than a nod. Murray nodded "yes." For once, things felt simpler.

Chapter 26.5i:
Smile, Slap 'Em and Lull 'Em

Jimmy seemed different. He was never sure of himself, but his jaunt, his half smile, and the folder he was holding on to seemed peculiar. Jake asked him, "Jimmy, everything okay? You seem a bit scattered. And, well, what's in the folder?" Jimmy said, "Tse has some important stuff for me, but I can't say." Jake laughed, "Jimmy, you just said." Jimmy looked mad, "Damn it Jake." Jake stopped. *What's wrong with Jimmy? Am I imagining this?* He said, "Hey Jimmy—what'd they give you?" Jimmy pulled the folder even closer. Jake said, "What's in the folder Jimmy?" Jimmy looked sad, angry, happy. Jake repeated, "Jimmy, what'd they give you? What's in the folder?" Jake assumed they must have given him a promotion, travel options, or more swag. Jimmy said, "Ok Jake—they gave me—look, they gave me— look here, ok, look here, more opportunity, look, I will lead the project." Jake grabbed the folder. There was a thin paper with a request for data. He didn't know how to tell Jimmy his thoughts. Jake said, "Jimmy, uhm, more responsibility, more work? To retrieve data?" Jimmy said, "No, more visibility…" Jake let him ramble, "You been talking to Tse, Cluster and HR eh?" Jimmy said, "They want me to be somebody Jake." Jake said, 'You are somebody Jimmy—you're Jimmy." Work took advantage of the fact that the individual was always searching for themselves. They synthesized enough purpose with need authority and fear to bind it together. They'd lulled Jimmy with a folder, and probably some swag. Jake thought, *what did they do to Jimmy?* He just couldn't shake it. They'd claim civilization—when all they did was take bestial behavior and label it, feed it a packaged item, feign some advancement. What happened to Jimmy almost happened to Jake, and Jake hated what he'd become at times. Hypocrisy was universal to everyone, but he hoped he had less of it in him. He had his times. He had been hurt and humiliated, and at times it haunted him still. The irony was there even was a time, where a small victory was achieved—it was before Cluster at some point—some Box-On-Top asked him on a performance review to rate himself. He was so used to hearing "you really think you deserve that?" that he defaulted to saying "average," and the Box-On-Top said, "I rated you above." Jake was embarrassed about being embarrassed. Here he was actually getting some praise, and he couldn't even accept it. Jake always fought back, even at his lowest. The same couldn't be said for others (i.e. Zach would have sold his soul even if no one was buying).

Jake must have been hallucinating. This must all be a dream. He must be imagining this.

Chapter 27:
Equity of Inequality

Some get more, some get less and most get lost. Why did Billy disappear? Why does any of it happen? Whoever asked for any products? Jake concluded that it was effort best spent not on the *why*, but on what to do about it at this point. And that, if changed enough times, can make life more manageable. One had to be cautious so as to not make the problem overly simple to the point where it wasn't as relevant, nor too big or unsolvable. Fixing the world—maybe figuring out a new system—too big. What snack to eat next—probably too small. Accept some facts that creatures are unfair and that these same creatures created the corporation, so work was unfair. Creatures who were greedier and more aggressive, who by construction kept each other in power, were more likely to create and run corporations. The whole system appropriated the employee for the system of created consumption and production, and that cycle had to exist. The displacement of anger did nothing other than displace anger.

It was one of the most dangerous crimes an individual could commit against themselves, to displace anger to a loved one or the innocent. Cynicism, anger, and not dreaming were all crimes against the self, a loved one, or the innocent. Jake was trying to push his feelings down. There were cities in other lands with corporations that were much harsher—stories of creatures throwing themselves from the tops of the highest floors. One could guarantee one thing. That no one was treated equally. That was the only guarantee from work, the work itself, and its various punishments, were the consistent parts. That was the argument of realities. Life might be more barbaric in some ways, more direct at times without the corporation, but mostly free. Imagine that, tribes that you picked, that weren't artificial, that you grew loyal to, and grew loyal to you, similar to that concept of family he'd heard about from ancient times. A message popped up on his screen. Jake thought, *is there no calm*? He responded to the message.

Jake let the other incoming messages go stale. Attention wasn't the only thing up for grabs; privacy was a pseudo-right and using it practically required an alibi. One couldn't even use the excretion chamber or call in sick without have to give a full diagnosis and detailed report. Messages of 'Out Sick' followed by the '…left hoof had a bunion…' and '…the malady of my stomach and that I ate too many snacks and can't stop the excretions…' The horror! How you had to describe every ailment, excuse everything, sometimes you had to appear happy and other times happier. What did all that amount to? More products, more consumption, but no real change in anything of value, with the outcome always being fewer connections amongst creatures, less time to spend for themselves, or discovery in this life. The corporate institution had no bars, so you could, in theory, break out or quit, but the entire social structure was set up in a way that your social value and purpose were limited and negative. Quit to where? Another job. How could you afford anything? Everything was transacted in units, and one would never make more than enough units. That is aside from losing the validation of society.

Jake didn't care, or need units to love, or feel humor, warmth, loyalty, or something manufactured. When your only expression was in your units and where you worked, it meant little, and arguably since you weren't an owner you had less to lose than to gain (although it never felt like that). It was a matter of probability, the creature making 50,000 units could lose 50,000 units, and was deathly scared of that, whereas the one making millions of units somehow did not have the same insecurity. The corporations made it difficult to be someone. Even in the limited time you spent away from work, your mind was tangled in the next task, next project, next fight to get up for. The individuals at the office could on occasion be friends, be good people, but most were not. They were out to get you on different levels, some implicitly, through their own self-serving ways, others because of survival, and some for the purposes of downright cruelty. Imagine if someone were to be a soldier, some would shy away and do it only in moments of need and defense, while others were sadists and happened to enjoy being soldiers. Some at work enjoyed the structure, the power, the control, the influence. It was twisted, and would suck you in; if you weren't in the machinery, who were you? Just an individual, presenting yourself only on your own name. Not Jake, of BLC Corp, of Team..., of Project..., of Manager.... How often do you identify yourself by the Box-On-Top? I work for ... or the team? I am part of the team.... But really you are just Jake. How could anyone introduce themselves as 'I am Jake, I don't work...', and to who? He would be in his singular existence. Like Stephan, the misfit. Jake's own mind couldn't separate that concept of identity and work; to not work was to be a misfit. There wasn't just Stephan. Orwell was there too: broken, misshapen, no real past, and certainly no future. Yahn was there. Alfonse, Floral. Some had been retired, some were born damaged. Society had little use for the damaged. Some couldn't pass their test in the brooding chambers, some were physically malformed.

All these thoughts Jake had, these "discoveries," this mental energy spent figuring out the system, were no doubt also discovered by every other thoughtful, rational employee. While all this was being done, time was moving. Time compounded, added, moved, was lost, and never returned. The units of time were just ways for organic creatures to "count" and refer to time, but it was never meant to be 'captured' or 'controlled.' Really—time couldn't be 'controlled.' Every day lost moves us closer to the end. Corporations were a controlled prison of sorts. Imprisoned by our need for validation, for units, for purpose, to use our time. A corporation claimed to give purpose, to create and hold up society. Like many lies and abuses, it came in gradual steps. Some parts of it, it could not control itself. Possibly if one or two corporations existed, or many small ones, maybe the dynamic would be different, but who's to know? Monopolies, oligopolies with a dash of small companies was the reality. No single corporation could be blamed, but greed unbridled with products unnecessarily built upon the backs, souls, and minds of individuals was owned by someone, mostly the owner and a small part the employee. Now if the species wanted to become vapid in soul and robotic in existence, maybe it was fine, but Jake doubted that's what the species wanted.

Joey was nearby in the break room. He always seemed reasonable. Jake said, "Joey!" Joey said, "Jake! Hey pal." Joey seemed a bit shaky. Jake said, "What's wrong Joey?" Joey said, "This Uniq-corn—Cluster promised me the promotion. I was promised!" Jake said sarcastically, "Uh, yeah, well promises are worth it." Joey said, "They promised all the knowledge of the world, a promise of titles, invites to meetings." Jake paused, "What world Joey?" Joey responded, "They are...they owe me...I did everything." Jake was confused, but said, "Ok, I have to leave." Joey kept talking to himself, "...I...turned...Billy." Jake stopped and walked back, "Wait what about Billy? Turned?

What did you turn? Did you say Billy?" Joey said, "I gave them..." Jake was confused, "Gave them what? I know we all give them time and work, but what can you do." Joey said, "No, Billy." Jake angrily yelled, "Joey! You gave them Billy? What does that even mean? What on Billy!" Joey said, "I told them about Billy." Jake said with apprehension, "What did you tell them about Billy? Were you following him?" Joey responded, "Look, Billy wasn't following the rules. He made the mistakes. I merely shared that with leadership." Jake finished, "I won't hear any more of this Joey...Good luck with your promotion. What mistakes? Who made the rules? Did he take an extra pad from the supply room? Eat an extra snack? Think for himself?" Jake walked off angrily. Uniq-corn, Cluster, Joey...the world of failed corporations. A weak but impish fool that squeals and a person with no ethics in actualization, effect and result were one and the same. But Jake thought, was Joey really that? Was it his fault or the system's, which promoted and allowed this kind of betrayal? Joey was a friend of Billy's. He couldn't even know that Billy was seeking independence. Billy had always said a quote to Jake, "A weak friend is worse than a strong enemy." Jake thought, *I think I understand now, better to see directly ahead of you an attacker than the unexpected stabs from those behind you, hidden and less defensible.*

Jake ran over to his desk, started collecting his belongings. He thought...well...now is the chance to go. To leave and escape. He had some people he wanted to say bye to. But he would drag them along in a possible wake of his departure. He had spent a lifetime thinking of the end, of demise, of the eventual retirement. That's what everyone worked towards: maybe a promotion, maybe a company transfer, but not much else would happen. There wasn't too much to be surprised by at work. It was a well-worn path. He'd contemplated what it all meant, the endless work, but the escape? What next? His gut churned. He had always depended on mind and logic. This corporate servitude was trained into you and not part of you; it took your soul and so you had to fight against it. He could not know what was on the other side. Jake had to come up with a plan. The plan would be...grab all the snacks he could, take some supplies, write down a few building contact numbers. Then, well, hmm, he would stay in his building. But then they would come to retire him. He couldn't retire this early, so maybe the Department of Lost Souls? Then they would humiliate him. Society would think him...him...unem...unemployed. Lazy...slothful. That he had no worth. He would also have no units. He'd barely skimp by on what he saved. There weren't any other ways really to earn units.

Chapter 28:
Failure is an Option

Jake stopped working as hard. He still didn't have a plan. He simply let the numbers round themselves. He let the sheets populate themselves. He still had to move the mechanical arms in the simulator, that could actually injure someone. He took more breaks. He thought *"what's in it for me?"* more often, and *"who benefits?"* more often... He threw out the old quotes he'd heard, "put in your time"... "it is what it is...we are just chopping wood" (whatever the hell that meant). He ignored the carrot and stick, no, no you were not going to make it—the odds were so low, and the cost of your soul too high. You had to say no at every stop, or the attrition of your soul would take place. Eventually there was no protective layer, and everything peeled back as an onion or occasionally sliced down the middle. Protect your onion, or brain, or whatever. It didn't matter, the metaphor or analogy, or quote. Protect yourself. Jake started thinking who cares if he was "unemployed," who cares what society thought of him? What society was this? The one that willingly let generations, and generations of its species die for the benefit of war machines, or because medicines using basic chemicals cost too much? There were villains, certainly, those who did nothing, and those who committed the atrocities, and the only victims were those who all this was committed against.

The corporate wars and deaths were of a non-corporeal nature, death by a thousand keyboard/touch pad (or whatever) entries, filings, hourly trackings that took place. Corporeal death could be counted, but the number of hearts and minds distracted and destroyed never would be recognized or enumerated. One could say corporations were the lesser of evils (of how many evils one could find) of governments and such in their indirect cause of death. Then again, it was corporations that turned their view away from the result, they supplied weapons, profited, and avoided helping anyone without intent (for rarely do things happen by coincidence). There were certain industries, defense ('suppliers of war'), finance ('legal robbery') that were morally bankrupt to the point that they could only survive off vampirism—sucking the soul, morality, and all units from any other company or individual. They were so close in the linkage of profit the only thing between them was the creatures—no actual products, rates on rates, loans on loans, or weapons that eliminated creatures instantly (albeit weapons required a bit more factory than finance).

These corporations had the benefits of individuals, limited liability, c-corp, s-corp, or whatever-corp, but had no responsibility. It took creatures to create the corporation and protect it, thinking they'd protect themselves—the elite creatures that is, those above the law, beyond the law, who made the law. Jake had learned more and more on his discreet library trips. There were more basic indecencies, the factories, the move from factories to cubicle farms, and so on. No one died in a cubicle farm, but the herd, and being treated as sheep was just the same (no disrespect to sheep). He told Jimmy to stop. He told Geraldine. He built himself up, tore himself down, got beaten all around, but was better, and different. He told Cluster "Not right now," "Can I get back to you?" and eventually he could say, "No," and that in itself was the most powerful statement. He did not feel the need to engage in politicking with Caelestis. He felt free. Feeling free was one of the most important things, although the reality was never completely there. Now even getting to feel free could not come without a cost and without risk. Cluster wanted to review his work. HR wanted to talk about Retirement and Loss. Zach, Kyle, Florian, and yes, even, Joey and the collaborators wanted to fight. You're dying anyway, retired or sent to the department of lost souls. Really, why was quitting not an option? I mean real quitting. Part of it was never going to be complete, so he would have to keep himself convinced that it was okay to walk away. Uniq-corn walked by in the hallway and said, "Hey Jake, I'd like to talk to you about something we chatted about." Jake was caught off guard. He didn't want to be 'nice,' he just wanted to be 'fair' to himself. He knew himself, and he was a good person. He did not know Uniq-corn, the extension of the corporation, but Uniq-corn approached him a in open-hoofed way, disarming Jake.

Uniq-corn, holding a folder said, "We've been talking." Jake couldn't stop looking at the folder. That old feeling of trauma was coming back. Maybe it never goes away. Once the scar has been made it never heals fully, but at least it's quicker to heal, and he knows he survives every time. The absolute beauty of life is that you survive. No one owns that life. To gain freedom of your time, will, and direction would take awhile. It wasn't in Jake's habit. Uniq-corn said, "Jake, you there?" Jake was daydreaming, "Uh yeah, all here." Uniq-corn said, "I propose we make you responsible for Geraldine, Jimmy, and a few staff, not a Box-On-Top yet, but some initial responsibilities. Oh, and we have some interesting projects coming our way." Jake said, "Well, very kind of you, can I think about it?" Jake didn't want to be tactful, but he felt he needed to be. Some passive and slow ways of saying no unfortunately still came back through habit. Uniq-corn responded, "You are lucky

Jake, take the offer." Uniq-corn continued, "You want the alternative?...It really is a shame you take everything personally." Ah classic, threat, with a mix of "this could go well," sure, manage his friends, what a gift. Carrot poisoned with a hollow inside and a stick the size of a bat to punish him. The vanity in the 'offer' was almost as insulting in that it wasn't an 'offer,' but was just a rephrasing of things to come. The hypocrisy, of course, was also that Jake was taking it personally. Uniq-corn said, "And one more thing, don't you want to be rich? Well-known? Renowned?" Jake said, "It all depends on what your definitions of those things are: rich in friends, in love, yes. Renowned, no." He was offering Jake hope and manipulation. Not much was left for Jake but to look into some options.

Survivalist work instinct kicked in, could he transfer? Maybe he could work at another company. Start over. No, no. He's been at other companies. Jake had tried. Multiple companies. They were all the same, the product changed, but the garbage in/garbage out factor remained the same. One could also escape to 'cheaper truths' and accept ways out. Imagination and theory are far more limitless than reality, physics and the tangible. It is cheaper to go back and forth on imagination and theory and 'what if' than to actually make change. Discussion was a great distractor, and sometimes less "expensive" to accept these "cheaper truths." But authentic truth brings with it the reality of the situation. Occasionally of course one can make a bad decision. It does happen. Jake has made bad decisions outside of work. For another time, and another story. Well, a little of that. Well, there might have been a few bad decisions. Hmm, maybe he thought he shouldn't pull the trigger and doubt crossed his path. Well, love. Eh. Definitely made the biggest mistake there. Jake knew she was the one. She had a beautiful smile and expressed the world with her eyes. Jake knew she was the one when he saw her. He could talk to her, and Jake sure could talk, so she was a saint to hear the verbosity that made him. Despite his wisdom, knowledge, and capabilities Jake couldn't see what he had in front of him at times. Her wit, temperament, her unadulterated, pure, unconditional love. Her intelligence…a once-in-a-lifetime person. But hey, mistakes are made. Costs are paid. Work, misplaced advice, the socioeconomics, all of it is a masquerade. Jake almost never had time to think about his own life, not really. He had focused so much on work, on 'career,' that word made him nauseous. He forgot some parts of life. There were no awards or amounts of units that could compensate him for where he was at. Even those with billions of units. At some point what could they buy, super powers, eternal life, unlimited security? No, no, they could not. And if they could ever get beyond certain limits, they wouldn't be creatures anymore, more like robots or some base form of life.

Jake couldn't only put the blame on corporations. He did have a hand in all this. He chose to participate. He chose to put himself in the environment where he contributed to the machinery. He had more choice than some ancestors that he read about in the library, the pure serfs. There was a clear ownership of the employee then. It wasn't danced around, and physical punishment seemed quite common. You go into debt, they put you in debtor's prison! You are born of a certain breed, you get hung! Not that the species could congratulate itself to say it has gotten here, I mean, so you get benefits now, great, and you get snacks…that you should be happy you don't get hung or flogged, but still have to be humiliated, is an advancement. The amazing intelligence and capability of one individual, and to imagine that collective species still ends up here is fairly unimpressive, but then again this will get me to thinking once more of nepotism and other cynical features that although maybe real, just don't seem to be worth the effort to think through. The truth was always there, it was in love, it was in creating real value, it was in true friendships, and happiness. But this wasn't a love story.

Chapter 29:
Peace...Almost

Jake was going to confront his manager, the oh-so-Great Box-On-Top, the ever-right, the never-ending fool. He didn't want to. He had to. Well, maybe, he didn't have to. Noooo, he had to. Jake's mind was running. Cluster was in the way. Jake was going to tell Uniq-corn, surely, the actual head—or Cluster's soon-to-be replacement. Or maybe it was Cluster. Didn't matter. Time flies when you're not having fun, having fun, or otherwise. Jake was trying to think of some project that changed his life, or some relationship at the office that made him a grander, better person. He was reaching for some meaning to this corporate life, This life was still young and was his, but he was looking into his pad, looking at his own reflection, gray hair, tufted, particularly gray around the muzzle, whiskers a bit jagged as well. He could remember projects but that didn't mean they had value. He could recall some names, faces, of the coworkers. He had to reach back for some memories. There were some awful ones, and most were just time spent.

Back to the moment Jake had to face. He had to go see management, or maybe he just walks off. No more distractions, no games, no stories, no false promises. Might as well tell one of them and consider it done or maybe just leave.

Jake decided to walk off; he stopped working. He moved towards his desk, then paused. Cluster was walking towards him.

Jake ignored him. Cluster said, "You thinking of going somewhere?" Jake thought to himself, *has Cluster become psychic? If so I think you're an idiot Cluster.*' Jake said, "Somewhere—you don't need to know." Cluster said, smiling evilly, "What did you say? Just say it again—I don't need to know?" Jake said, "You don't need to know what I do with my life." Cluster was confused, "What life? Jake, your life is right here...at the office." Jake started walking away. Cluster said, "Jake, Jake, hey Jake...fix that behavior quick. This is not a wise decision...Listen, best case, we'll call you negligent...come back..." Cluster continued and muttered, "You damn animal Jake, you spineless...you could..." Jake kept walking and yelled, "We are all animals Cluster...don't make yourself feel different. And by the way I'm not an invertebrate." Well, that escalated quickly. An animal. Not a corporate creature. A corporeal soul perhaps. Before becoming a corporate retiree and being a retiree of choice. I'm an animal first, in between and last. Work is a practical matter. It is not a reason for existing. The nature of organic creatures is to attach worth and happiness and emotion to people and to events. Corporations take that nature and manipulate it. "Work," the term, and the verb become owned by the corporation. The skill is to learn to detach. Abstract. He knew he had to act. *Be the pack leader Jake,* he told himself, even if it's a pack of one. The environment would not change, and he did not want to change within the environment. It was easier for him to change, of course. He had the power, the knowledge to continue to survive it, but he just didn't want to make that choice. He would take a more barren life, disconnected, scorned, or whatever the costs were. Corporations would claim to own anything they could: life, death. Tse had told him once, "We own your soul Jake." Jake knew better. Even death was fairer. Even death showed no discrimination.

Somewhere beyond organic matter, blood weaving in tissue and cells blending together, between the borders and limits that make the individual, beyond their intelligence, was the base for construction of emotion, perhaps the soul, perhaps something else. That emotion always was there, that 'gut instinct' or intelligence or push. Take a being and deconstruct them, could one separate the various components? And even if someone were to artificially capture these triggers of emotions, combine them, apply them externally to the body, and study them would you capture that emotion? There would always be a pull for freedom. When overwhelmed by cheap accolades and acknowledgments, controlled through fear, societal identity, and other methods that pull for freedom, one could be subdued but never lost. The role of philosophers, theologians and scientists were all dedicated to some aspect of this translation, some interpretation mapping and the deconstruction of gut instinct and emotion. How would the corporations discover such things? Even if they could discover them, how could they take such discoveries and give them purpose? They only had proven to mutilate, stimulate, subdue and compound but never truly drive the individual from the point of sincere emotion and truth. Jake had to make a decision, or really, stick to the same decision. Jake had decided to walk—to free himself. He had to go to his place—quickly, gather his things, and take off. One of the rules of life should be never reveal your next move. Maybe he'd made a mistake by advertising his discontent and wanting to leave. Well. Too late for that.

Peace wasn't going to be in the form of material indulgence, or the drudgery of work, or in games, but instead in personal freedom, in the ability to stand by your own identity. To de-program. Jake didn't need science, advisors, or society to tell him what to do next. His good and developed, neural, organic, top-of-the-line mind could make its own decisions.

Chapter 30:
Not All Dogs go to Heaven

The hunt begins. The drones were sweeping the area. This couldn't be announced. The corporations were hunting him but couldn't advertise this at the office. This deviant and his deviation couldn't go unanswered. It also couldn't go uncaught and unpunished. What signal would this send, that animals can just walk off? That they wouldn't be tagged for the Department of Lost Souls—that they would just, define themselves? That they could throw off shackles, remove target objectives, and quit the chase? No. Jake had departed from protocol. Talk about a choice, between being lulled and de-fanged.

Jake hadn't had much time. He'd grabbed the book, many snacks, some limited memorable items he had. He had the map, and he'd carefully begun his trek to the library. It was quite daunting even leaving the building. It felt like a lifetime, but he had escaped. He'd also painfully broken apart the pad on his arm—some temporary swelling and then some psychological withdrawal of seeing the lights blink on his arm go out. He had thought of some of his friends—Jimmy, Geraldine—but really, he had to escape. He would have left them a proper note, but no time and better not to be traced to them for now.

Purpose. This substance cannot be measured in units nor discovered. Deeper than culture, further than proofs, removed from deductions and inference, from observation of science, from this or that and whatever other process takes something and pumps out the truth. Take the existence of atoms—one did not need to prove their existence for them to exist. In truth, in honesty, in sincerity, they exist. The failure of the organic creature is in always requiring and needing proof, is the inability to believe in things that don't exist to the senses or in the imagination. Falseness only exists when one refuses to accept truth. Truth existed independently on its own, it didn't need things to be false or a dichotomy. It was anchored in itself. When one buries truth under a layer of ignorance to save the soul from having to face that which requires facing, the individual does it to save the remaining amount of sanity. But confronting that stark layer of ignorance and teasing out the truth are the only ways to freedom. In other words, allowing ignorance is arguably one of the worst types of lies. It puts you in a limbo. Sometimes if it's mixed with a bit of truth, it's even more dangerous.

Time, time, time, was the other issue, not the other opportunity. The only parts of existence that should be passive are the autonomic functions. Everything else should have to be actively decided, planned, and lived, whether in the present or the future. To learn to fast, to learn to forgive oneself. Jake was going to plan his life. There was no traversing the past, nor was there jumping into the future, but he must live in the moment. Jake was going to simply live more. There was right and wrong. The corporation, the animals, would tell you what was right and wrong. They pushed their culture. But Jake was free. He wasn't going back. He had spent enough time running off and fighting unnatural predators. Better to die with time on your side, than time having moved past you. He let go of the work identity, so he could just be Jake, and then rebuild Jake as Jake the entrepreneur, or Jake the adventurer or Jake the shepherd…well, anyway, that could be figured out later, but he could just be Jake for now, the person he wanted to be.

Jake began reading about things he only dreamed of. He found some books on survival methods (useful books, and even more useful methods). He began scavenging for food at different times, for water from different places so as to avoid any possible capture by drones. He built some basic tools, some bedding in the library and patched together some of his clothes. He read about more and more things every day, from biology, to economics, to space travel. Take the eye, the organic top-of-the line camera, neural circuitry that enables contrast, color-analysis, film, and filter, and take a meaty being with no vision to one of vision. From the early times Jake's ancestors would wake up in packs to hunt and search for prey. Everyone who thought themselves untouchable were only untouchable until they weren't—this was divine law beyond even the corporation.

Jake learned about history, more and more. He would feel the pangs of loneliness from time to time, but also the pleasure of being alone in his thoughts. If society was more apt, or similar to some previous ones there would be families, for example. Someone to love you unconditionally and plainly. You could have your family, assuming society was built on families ahead of units, products, services. Sure, you could empower them or enrich them with the previous, but the value of society came down to the family, and how it treated itself and other families. *You're not alone in being alone, and you're not alone in pain* thought Jake, *but one step ahead was one step further from the past*. The family would be the first citizen, and the imagined version of what a corporation was would be a tool to merely supply creatures.

Things build over time in various traumatic bits and some just minimal bits, but it happens over time (because time is our only other dimension) that moves us 'forward' or 'backward' (in our minds) whether we choose to be moved or not. Jake had deplored spending any iota of extra time in any building, but somehow the library felt like a comfortable place. Here he believed life and time to be valuable. He believed existence was valuable. Now he could act on all these thoughts. He tinkered with his own ideas and devices (and created a few near-disasters). He worked on the creative arts: painting, drawing, and writing. He wandered around and mapped new buildings and some interesting tunnels under the library that would connect to different buildings. If he needed to, he could continue to explore through there. He would occasionally get old memories of pain and trauma from the corporation, Box-On-Top, the role. But he would remind himself to let go and focus on the opportunities ahead of him. To also one day help more like him, maybe like Jimmy and Geraldine, maybe even help creatures like Zach to value time and life. Jake was also more in touch with nature. He'd found plants thought long gone. Maybe if it had been known they were left they could be harnessed for possible marketable value. He'd found materials of old that seemed to have no purpose, such as robotic parts, and he started using those to assemble a robot. With enough books, and knowledge, and a lot of electricity, he'd power something, make a robot companion, or even an employee. Jake laughed. He'd eventually look for love again. Jake looked into a shiny object, he read about this thing—called a 'mirror.' He looked at himself. His age was just chronological—his spirit was free to explore, to face challenge, and recover from it. He had challenges coming up, but he would face them. He'd seek real purpose.

It could have been worse, Jake thought. He was never "set." He was never on the fast track, as no one really was. That in itself might have been a blessing. He would have still ended up here. The difference is he would've run out of time if he'd shown up later. Jake was no hero, nor did he care to be one. He was no savior, nor did he care to be one. His path was not to exert that which pleases others, or to consume things, or to live on emotions alone, or to avoid fears. Jake didn't know what it all meant yet, and he knew he would never know. Life couldn't be lived looking in a rear view. One could reason, arbitrate, but you would never know the future. Jake would never isolate, extract and understand every aspect of life and that was in itself great. There was always mystery, never complete control, but more than that in the confined realities of the corporation. "Live in the present, grow into the future. For society, freedom, existence, life and happiness," was Jake's new motto.

You go from nothing to something—and all the while you would seek wisdom and hope to retain innocence. It was natural. Value is what you give it. That is a freedom in itself. The corporate animal was the last vestige of the industrial revolution and the beginning of a corporate creature. Corporations expedited many discoveries and things, but what was the rush, as if it wouldn't have been discovered otherwise?

Jake wanted to just be a creature again. He wanted to be able to learn from his own base, senses, and investigations, or from the pure derivations of knowledge. Time was whatever you make it. Jake learned a lot more on matters of the soul, on cooking, eating, sleeping, thinking, art, history, spirit and purpose; he was finding his purpose. He learned to expose his weaknesses more, to see himself as part of the group as well as to be an individual and to seek actions that improved life around him. He found a hero in himself and a purpose in worshipping the one and only God. He had picked up archaic skills like farming and building by hand. He did not need validation nor units. And he wanted family, to draw, and to design a society. And of course, he still wanted chips, but he chose his purpose. Everyone could choose his or her purpose, and everyone should.

9 ✓
10
11 ✓
13 ✓
15
17
21
25 ✓
26
38 ✓
47 ✓
67 ✓

185 ✓
192 ✓
199 ✓
201 ✓
204
205 ✓

Made in the USA
Middletown, DE
05 September 2019